IF ONLY

TWO LIVES, ONE STORY.

BOUND BY FEAR, DIVIDED BY CIRCUMSTANCE

A Novel By

Bethany Lunney

THE BOOK CHIEF

IGNITE YOUR WRITING

Published by The Book Chief Publishing House 2025
(a trademark under Lydian Group Ltd)
Suite 2A, Blackthorn House, St Paul's Square,
Birmingham, B3 1RL
www.thebookchief.com

Cataloguing in Publication Data is available from the British Library.

ISBN:

Book Cover Design: Naeema / Abu Bakar Javed
Editing / Proofreading: Craig Smith (CRS Editorial)
Typesetting / Formatting / Publishing: Sharon Brown

Published by The Book Chief

Table of Contents

Introduction

If Only is a gripping and deeply emotive tale of two young lives, Zoe and Ellen, navigating their personal battles within a world that often feels unkind and overwhelming. Though separated by circumstance, their stories intertwine in ways neither could have foreseen.

Zoe Brown, a thoughtful and self-aware teenager, struggles with the weight of living in a world that constantly demands conformity. Battling anxiety, feelings of isolation, and the daily pressures of fitting in, Zoe's journey reveals the hidden struggles of countless young people who feel unseen in their own lives. Through her humour, resilience, and sharp observations, she invites us into her world—a place where insecurities and longing for acceptance collide.

Ellen Maclaren, on the other hand, faces a much harsher reality. Forced to grow up too fast, Ellen bears the burden of protecting her baby sister from a chaotic and abusive home. Her life is a testament to courage, love, and the human will to survive, even in the darkest of circumstances.

At its core, *If Only* explores themes of identity, resilience, and the profound impact of human connection. It sheds light on the challenges faced by those grappling with mental health, trauma, and social isolation, while also showcasing the strength and hope that can emerge from adversity.

Through alternating perspectives, Bethany Lunney masterfully weaves a story that is raw, heart-wrenching, and ultimately uplifting. As readers, we are called to walk beside Zoe and Ellen—to share their fears, their triumphs, and their dreams.

This is a story of two lives, bound by fear yet brimming with hope, reminding us all that even in the bleakest moments, there is light to be found.

Chapter 1

Zoe

In many of the books I've read, I have found things start well before progressing into a full-blown dilemma that ends happily ever after. I, however, am going to be real from the outset. If you like to read completely happy books, I'd recommend you stop now.

My life felt desolate and bleak in that moment. I didn't know who I was or who I was meant to be, not understanding why I was so different from everyone else, and why everything was a struggle. My name is Zoe Brown and I am going to take you through my journey. It's not all a rainbow of acceptance and maths with geeky-looking glasses. For a start, I don't wear glasses and I cannot stand maths; it is the worst subject invented in my opinion! I mean, we're expected to calculate pointless numeric formulas with letters mixed in while we could be putting our energy into tackling the climate crisis or fighting for girls in Afghanistan to get an education.

Did you know there are 100 types of gerbil? (At least that's what Google tells me.) Amazing, isn't it? Gerbils aren't like most rodents. They aren't nocturnal, and they clean themselves in sand instead of water. They can survive way more than a week without drinking and they dig tunnels underground. That's what makes them so interesting; more so than a hamster, a goldfish, a rat or a budgie. And much more interesting than a rabbit or a guinea pig (though if we had the space, I would happily house all these creatures).

Sometimes that's how I feel. Different from all the others on the inside, though on the surface I appear 'normal'. There are times I think people like me may be the best actors of all, because we have to do it day after day. I keep searching for an answer, a light at the end of this callous tunnel I am suffocating in, but I can't find one. Often in bed at night I feel like screaming. Everything is such hard work and all my effort is in vain because I fail to grasp the one thing I long for: acceptance. It's not that difficult, is it?

In the wild, a gerbil's fur is the same colour as the desert that surrounds them, for camouflage. In pet shops, gerbils are available in many colours. Their fur can protect them from sunburn in the desert, but my skin can't protect me from society, and my skull can't protect me from the constant drilling of anxiety I feel in my head, always overthinking everything, having no control of the thoughts that possess me.

It was break time when I discovered it. My worst nightmare. Anyone else wouldn't think twice. Anyone else would be excited. Not me. I had to pretend. That's all I ever seemed to do back then: mask.

"Hey, Zoe! Come sit with us!" called Ava. I smiled and walked over, trying to blend into the background; slip behind the cracks. They were all talking about some

TikTok dance craze. I didn't understand. Why didn't I understand?

Overall, girls my age just seem to want to talk about make-up, boys and how awful their lives are. Why was everyone so vacuous? I always pretended to like the same things as they did, but to be honest it confused me why the length of your skirt matters so much when there are wars going on and people starving to death in other countries. I never quite knew what to say and when to laugh.

"Look!" said Ava, and she demonstrated some twirly dance, wiggling her hips in time to some tune. It wasn't that good, despite everyone cheering. Ava was supposedly my best friend, if you like to call it that. We had known each other since Reception and had always been 'best friends'. I couldn't help worrying now, though. I was scared it was my fault. I wasn't exciting enough any more. I didn't wear make-up. I wasn't on TikTok. I smelled. So many theories; none the true answer.

"Come join me, Zoe!" she said, pulling me off my seat abruptly, making me lose my balance in the process. I shook her off. They all started a pathetic 'kiss-marry-kill' game, giggling and gasping. I tried to keep my expressions in unison with theirs.

"Hey, Zoe, would you rather..." Ava started, beaming, about to string off a list of candidates.

"I'm going to the loo," I said, and shuffled off before I could be embarrassed.

When I looked back, Ava was raising her eyebrows at me, and I saw Emily whisper something and all the girls giggled. I heard the word 'weird' and shut my eyes, trying to keep the emotion in.

Why does it hurt so much if you know it's true?

Everyone says that words can't hurt you, or 'it's just a joke'. But in my experience, the sheer agony of one word can throb just as much as any broken bone. It didn't help that Ava was involved. I know this must sound petty and pathetic, but as I said before, she was meant to be my best friend. We used to have sleepovers most Fridays where we would do our homework companionably, sharing a packet of Doritos while scribbling away. Then later, we would eat oven pizza (occasionally a takeaway if we were lucky), a margherita with pineapple chunks, because that was our favourite. It would always be at my house, though. The thought of sleeping on a strange-smelling, half-deflated blow-up airbed made my stomach flip. Ever since halfway through Year 8, the sleepovers have fizzled out. Ava was always 'busy'. She did invite me round to her place once for a sleepover with Emily. This time it was me who was 'busy'.

Why did I fear sleepovers, parties and shopping trips so much?

You know why, Zoe.

All girls care about is being cool and boys. All the girls, an army of similarities. It is so tedious.

I was just about to walk into the cubicle when I stopped. There was a poster on the door.

'We are delighted to announce the Year 9 residential to Ashwood Forest!

This is a really good opportunity to celebrate the start of your GCSE course.

27th - 30th September

Compulsory for Year 9s.

More information will be given by your tutors.'

I stood reeling at the door, anxieties filling my head. In the background there was a picture of children kayaking on a river surrounded by trees. There was no way I could stay at a residential. I couldn't stay away from my home, my bed, my pillow, my smells, the gerbils, the dog, my mum and the coconut-shampoo-smelling bathroom. I remembered all previous sleepovers. All starting with me laughing, telling mum I was nearly a teenager and didn't need to bring my old teddy 'Mr Snuggles' with me for my sleeping bag, and ending in the middle of the night, with me crying in hysterics and mum driving there to take me back home, while everyone else was confused and wary of inviting me back. I felt angry that my whole life was controlled by anxiety. Every day being misunderstood. Every second worrying whether I should laugh or not; what my response should be. I always seemed to do everything wrong.

For most people, this probably seems pathetic. A soon-to-be 14-year-old getting worked up over a few nights away, having fun with her friends. How can I explain it? It was anything but fun.

Why am I so different?

You know why, Zoe; you just won't admit it.

Chapter 2

Ellen

"Don't cry, mum," I said, yet again.

"He's not worth it."

Mum was drunk. You could always tell when she was. I can sense if she's happy or sad from a mile away. Her black mascara ran down her face in grey trickles and her words were slurred. I don't think she even knew this man's name, but then, sometimes, I'm not sure she knows who I am, she's so drugged. But then, weren't all mothers? I knew my mum was a kind, loving mother who cared for me very much, and I was an extremely difficult girl. This lie that I always told myself was becoming more difficult to believe with each passing day.

Every crumpled spliff.

Every dried bottle.

Mum was constantly down at the pub with men, most of whom she'd never see again. I got left alone, but it's fine like that. I used to get scared, but mum said I was being selfish and that most people my age were left while their parents went out.

I don't know why but I love her, even though it's more like I'm the mum sometimes; a lot of times, actually.

But she is my mum, no matter what.

I heard wailing. It was my baby sister, Mabel. I'm not sure mum loves her either, despite her being her daughter.

I'm her daughter and she doesn't act like she loves me. I don't understand it. Emotions are all mixed up.

"She needs feeding," I told mum, abruptly.

"That bloody baby, just bloody wailing all day. It makes my head ache, and don't you take that tone with me, Ellen." She didn't actually say 'bloody'. She substituted it for coarse swearing beginning with 'f', the callous words shattering the air around us as tears filled my eyes in sheer pain for Mabel. She went over to her. Mabel stopped crying and looked up hopefully at mum with her big, beautiful blue eyes, the soft brown fluff of hair on her head just like a duckling's fluff. Her little starfish hands reached up; the skin soft with each nail perfectly placed.

"Shut the fucking hell up!" screamed mum into her soft little face. Poor Mabel's delicate expression screwed up in fear and she started crying again, fresh tears running down her soft, thin cheeks. I ran over, picked her up and started comforting her.

"It's not her fault, mum! She needs feeding!" I begged her.

"Well go heat some milk up for her then!" she slurred, flatly. The only milk we had was revoltingly curdled.

I often wondered if every child's life was like this. You might think I was a pretty stupid girl, living this way and thinking that everybody lived the same.

But when you've grown up for years in a reality, life just becomes a habit; a quirk you assume everyone has because you're taught no different.

No. Stop being selfish, Ellen. Poor mum has had a lot on her mind and all you've done is be difficult.

But I couldn't stop.

"She needs the special formula. Give me a fiver and I'll go and buy some now. Shop milk will upset her tummy."

"Go and buy it yourself then" she snarled, with droplets of spit landing on me.

"Mum, please! Where is the rest of the child benefit?" I begged her. Then I looked around at all the empty bottles and cans on the squalid carpet. Mum had plenty of child allowance...that she had obviously spent on drink!

Why hadn't I taken more when I'd snaffled the notes to buy baby things?

I assumed I had got enough powdered formula to last.

"She needs feeding!" I said, again, feebly.

Then another thought struck me so hard I reeled.

How could I have been so stupid?

I had got the last lot of formula about a week ago, trusting mum would follow my instructions to feed Mabel while I was working my shift at the pub.

"When was the last time you fed her?"

Mum ignored me, staring blankly at the wall, her eyes wild and glazed.

"Go and get mummy's tobacco tin, Ellen. Top drawer, beside my bed," she slurred.

I ignored her, terrified.

"Mum, have you given her the formula today like we said, remember? You have to give it to her three times a day! MUM!"

I shook her, terrified, my heart racing.

I'd been at work all day so I couldn't keep an eye on her.

Mum had a friend at the local pub who, on the quiet, had let me work there for the last year or so, unloading crates of bottles and washing glasses during the day. I had to say I was 14...but I would be next summer. My days at school were getting scarce by this point. I had begged mum to let me go back after she pulled me out completely, but she had reminded me, firmly: "Going to school doesn't pay the bills!"

Mum also used to work at The Fox and Horse - the local pub - but then started flirting with her boss and her drug dependency took her away from me. That's how Mabel came to be. I don't know who *my* dad is. Sometimes, when mum would have a bad day, I would daydream about this father figure. He would take me to the park and hold my hand. Read me stories. *Love* me.

Mum never wanted a baby, but there was nothing I could do. She wouldn't go to hospital for the birth. I had to lay towels in the bath and help her, though I was terrified. And then I didn't know what to do with Mabel once she was born. I still remember that night with shivers. Mum wouldn't help and just kept whining on about Bill (Mabel's dad). Mabel would have died if I hadn't ran to the next-door neighbour's house. She beat me for that too. I remember vividly sitting on the edge of the bath, rocking Mabel's soft, warm baby body. Whispering into her ear, "I love you", feeling the blood on my back trickling down my spine. I had to make sure she knew she was loved. Mum didn't show her any sign of affection. I didn't want her to grow up like me. I couldn't let her live in this reality too.

Mabel was screaming again. Despairing, yearning howls.

"Mum, please give me some money! She *needs* feeding!" I begged again, looking at Mabel's skinny, vulnerable body. I saw how her ribs stuck out; her tiny fists clenched as she sucked at them desperately. Her arms and legs looked as if they were about to snap, yet her tummy was bloated. I picked her up and rocked her in my arms.

I felt my ears ring as the neighbours thumped on the thin walls and swore, cursing for peace.

"And you can shut up, you pious bastards!" slurred mum, hurling an empty bottle at the wall. I winced as the glass shattered jaggedly on impact, but it was nothing new, as mum often had cursed rows with other tenants.

"I love you, Mabel," I whispered, trying to soothe her from the noise, before turning back to mum.

"Please, mum, please!" I pleaded.

But mum just ignored me, inhaling deeply on her cigarette.

Mabel was still screaming.

"Get that thing to shut the hell up, Ellen!" she yelled at me.

"Mum, she's crying because she's bloody hungry!" I screamed in despair.

Then I stopped, startled. I had never shouted at mum before. No wonder mum hated me. The banging and cursing from the neighbours intensified.

"How dare you take that tone with me!" she roared, as she rose to her feet, staggering.

"I'll teach you a lesson!"

She grabbed my arm before I could run, wrenching me towards her. I realised I was still holding Mabel and she tumbled out of my arms on to the hard wood floor, screaming.

"Mabel!" I gasped, trying to go to her, but mum still grasped me tight. This was all my fault.

Sometimes, even now, I realise I carry that same knot of guilt in the depths of me. What might have been if I could have run a little quicker; held a little tighter?

"I'm going to teach you a lesson that you'll never forget," she hissed.

"I'm...sorry...mum!" I wept breathlessly, before she slapped me full across the face. I reeled and tumbled to the floor. I felt the blood dripping from my nose, and collapsed, sobbing. Then I remembered. Mabel was still howling on the floor.

"Mabel!" I gasped. I tried to get up, but my legs were too weak. Mum got there first.

"Please mum, NO!" I sobbed desperately.

But she wouldn't listen.

She shook and shook Mabel, took her head in her hands, yanking it backwards and forwards, shaking and shaking her.

I could no longer hear the yearning sobs. In fact, I couldn't hear anything; the room was whirling and flashing around me.

"Mabel!" I wheezed desperately, forcing myself to stand up and go to her, while the room spun around me.

Mabel wasn't moving. Her body lay motionless on the floorboards; her face blue, with mouth open. Blooded saliva was dripping garishly from her open mouth.

"Oh, Mabel," I wept uncontrollably, taking her body in my arms. Mum had passed out on the floor. I ran to the phone and dialled 999.

Chapter 3

Zoe

I couldn't concentrate at all that day. The word 'residential' was spinning around my head like an annoying fly that won't buzz off. I thought of all the sleepovers I'd ever had and shivered. I found myself asking questions that became louder and louder as they attacked me.

What if I'm sick on the residential?

What if I wet the bed?

What if I don't even have a bed to sleep on?

What if... What if... What if...?

I flicked to the back of my chemistry book and started to draw Sally, our dog, in the margins to distract myself. Sally running, Sally sleeping, Sally snuggled on the sofa with me, Sally-

"Zoe!" came the booming, all-too-familiar voice of Mr Macclesfield. Unfortunately, he was my chemistry teacher as well as form tutor.

I was startled and accidentally put a line through my drawings.

"What would I get if I mixed iron filings and hydrochloric acid?"

"Erm..." I said, trying to make sense of the weird scribbles on the whiteboard. I realised I hadn't been listening to a word of what he had been saying. "I'm not sure, Sir," I said, ducking my head to hide my blush.

"I expected as much. You need to pay attention, Zoe! I've had enough of your daydreaming!" I nodded, hating being told off and really did try to pay attention, but before I could help myself I was already lost in a world of my own.

Late that night, I lay awake in bed, shaking. I was going on the residential tomorrow, or today, whichever way you want to look at it. I tried to explain to mum, but she didn't understand. She told me it would be 'such fun' and 'I'd soon not be worried'. Little chance of that. It felt like wasps were flying like racing cars around my brain. I clasped my head as every thought continuously punched me.

What if I'm sick on the coach?

What if the mattress is lumpy?

What if all the food is horrid?

What if I miss home?

What if I get ill?

What if my mum or dad die while I'm away?

What if I'm the reason they died?

What if there are germs in the toilet?

I had tried talking to dad as well, but he just rubbed the back of his head where the scalp showed, and said: "Talk to your mum, Zoe. I can't be doing with your tantrums right now, darling."

I wished I lived by the sea. All I could hear were cars and noise and people and roads. I tried to make up sounds of country and waves, but I had always found it hard to imagine vividly. I remembered last summer when we went on holiday to Wales. I always had to wear armbands in the sea with dad because I couldn't swim, but it was worth it. The cool, icy shock of the sea biting your toes when you first get in, and the joy of being uprooted on a bodyboard - though there was always a tiny niggling fear of a crab or jellyfish. I would never let the water get above my waist, terrified of going out of my depth and been swept away forever.

Apart from that, most of my worries lay at bay, yet I could never get away from them. They would always be there, whenever, and whatever I did. A knotted ball of rocks in my stomach which attacked constantly.

I knew we were doing canoeing at this place, but even in the photo on the poster the river looked dirty and foul. Another bout of anxiety.

What if I murder my mum?

What if I pray for Sally to die while I'm away?

What if I drown and die?

So many 'what ifs'.

If you have never personally experienced severe OCD, you probably think these questions are a load of nonsense. For me, they were so real. A choking, strangling thundercloud in my head, every day convincing me so many phantom, awful terrors were genuine.

That night, I eventually fell asleep in my bed with the sound of mum and dad's breathing in the next room and the traffic outside, silently screaming under the surface.

In the morning, mum woke me up super early with a breakfast tray of my usual orange juice and cereal, along with a travel sickness tablet. She had made sure to put the milk in a little jug adjacent to the cereal, remembering my hate of soggy cornflakes.

"Here you go, my darling," she said, smiling.

I buried my face into her soft brown hair and breathed in her 'mum smell'. I loved my mum so much. I couldn't leave her. "You are going to be absolutely fine, and you'll have fun with Ava."

I wasn't so sure.

Images flashed through my head. At primary school, Ava and I had been so-called best friends, as I said, but now she always looked embarrassed when I came over, and she made it plain she preferred a girl called Emily. I really tried not to mind and did everything just like they did.

Emily had long, thick blonde hair and two shiny piercings in each ear along with a hoop in her cartilage. Her lips were glossy and her make-up that she applied every day was immaculate. She had never actually been nasty to me (I didn't think so anyway), but she always whispered and giggled with Ava whenever I came near and often raised her eyebrows at me. Her skin was another matter, so milky and smooth like rosebuds; mine is awful, pale and puny with pimples, worse luck. I once tried to apply make-up properly - foundation, highlighter and all that nonsense - but it felt so stiff and sticky on my face I washed it off almost immediately.

"Hmm," I said, munching. The cereal was good and the milk extra creamy.

"Mum, do I really have to go?" I asked, playing with the milk at the bottom of the bowl, spooning it up and streaming it back into the bowl.

"Look, Zoe, we've been over this. You're going to have such fun - and don't play with the milk like that! Look, you've spilt it on the tray. Why don't you drink it?"

"Mum, it's got bits of cornflake in it," I said, pretending to retch.

"That's enough, Zoe! If you're finished you need to get dressed." Mum sighed, but I could tell she wasn't really cross.

I reluctantly slid out of the safe, warm cocoon of my bed to start the day. I laid out my clothes and trainers. Then I quickly had a shower, anxiously scrubbing at my skin. A little soap went into my eyes. Maybe that's why the tears fell.

I later went into the kitchen and tied my straggly black hair into a ponytail. Dad came stumbling into the kitchen, rubbing his eyes and yawning. I went over to hug him. His nightshirt was still warm from his and mum's bed, and he smelled comfortingly of sleep and sweat.

"Go and show them, baby pigeon!"

He always called me that, especially when I was sad. I'm not sure where it originated from, but I was happy to oblige and did a few shaky 'coo' noises.

"Come on, Zoe, we've really got to go," said mum, looking at the kitchen clock.

"Wait! Just one more thing!" I shouted.

I ran into mum's room and picked up her oldest stripy top and thrust it into my bag. Then I quickly raced up to my room and tried to give each gerbil a quick, loving stroke goodbye - well, apart from Luna. I think she must have some anger issues because she bites me if I dare stroke her! I also went to Sally, our black Lab, who is quite old and grey now, though no less loving. I crawled into her dog bed and breathed in the warm tang of her fur. She looked up at me with her deep, brown eyes, and thumped her tail. Sometimes I wished I was a dog. They don't have to worry.

"ZOE!" screamed mum. I sighed, gave Sally one more kiss on her damp nose, picked up my bag and ran downstairs. Mum hugged me tight, told me I was very special and brave, and handed me a flask of hot cocoa to take with me (the only hot drink I tolerated). I set off for school along the grimy pavements, trying to keep my head high, a cool autumnal breeze nipping at my face as I tried to avoid the cracks.

I didn't feel brave when I stepped into the playground. Year 9 boys were darting around playing a daft game of footy, Apple EarPods shoved lazily into their ears as they kicked the squalid football around the playing court. Suitcases lay around the concrete and teachers scurried around with clipboards. I saw James too, one of the more 'half-decent boys', as mum would say. I couldn't exactly call him my friend. Anyhow, girls are never friends with boys, but he was in my lessons and we were always 'matey' with each other. I found it so much easier to get on with boys and have banter.

I was startled as a horrid whistle sound made a wave across the playground. Mr Macclesfield, my form tutor, glared and glowered. I hated him and he hated me. He always had a way of making me feel small and humiliated, but subtly enough that he always got away with it.

"Year 9! Stop acting like you're aged nine! Enough of this childish behaviour, or you'll be sitting next to me on the coach."

Mr Macclesfield bellowed in the direction of the gang of boys, all of whom abruptly stopped playing football and whipped out their EarPods, standing to attention. He pointed to the school's logo; Cradisfield High School, with the motto: 'Work is passion'.

I never fully understood the name as there are no fields in south-east London, just traffic. I yearned for the peace and animals of the countryside. The seaside would be best. Not somewhere like Brighton, though. Somewhere calm and serene, where I could be peaceful and alone.

"Now, make an orderly line and fill up the coach back to front."

I looked to stand with Ava but she was with Emily, both of them on their phones using their bags as cover. I started crying without realising. It wasn't just fear, it was all the noise and everything being out of routine.

Zoe, copy everyone else, you don't need a routine. You're not a...

"Year 9! Line up in pairs and make an orderly queue! Now!"

I waited. My eyes closed, trying to block out reality. I knew what would happen. It always did. I looked desperately to Ava, but she just pretended not to see me, giggling and spluttering with Emily. I waited some more.

"Zoe Brown! Where is your partner?" Mr Macclesfield boomed.

"I...I don't have one," I spluttered.

"You don't have a partner?" he announced, loud enough for the whole of London to hear. Then he bent closer, so only I could hear him.

"Well, that's a surprise, isn't it?" he smirked. I closed my eyes, willing the ground to swallow me up.

Mustn't cry. Mustn't cry. Mustn't cry.

—

I had to go right to the front of the line; the only one without a partner.

What was wrong with me? Why does nobody like me?

You know why, Zoe.

I took a last gulp of fresh, icy air before getting on to the coach. It was hot and congealed with an overly pungent smell of travel, sweat, old sweetness and a bit of sick. I knew I would have to sit near the front. Anxiety didn't help the queasy situation, and a long journey to Ashwood Forest would not be pleasant. I sat in the frontmost seats - well, nearly the front, behind half a dozen form tutors and staff.

Mr Macclesfield came charging up the stairs on to the coach.

"You, Zoe! Don't you listen? I said to fill the coach up from the back."

I did listen. I tried to speak, but all the words knotted painfully in my throat.

I trudged to the seats at the back, alone, and watched happy, chatty people get on. All I wanted was to be in my safe, cosy home. I still hoped somebody might come and sit by me. Nobody came. I felt truly neglected and kept looking hopefully at anyone nearby to fill the empty seat. Anybody. Nobody came.

Why didn't anyone want to sit with me?

I waved at Ava, desperate not to lose the sliver of friendship we had left, but she nudged Emily and pretended not to have seen me. They sat in the middle, with loads of other girls. When the coach was running, they started recording a TikTok video behind their seat, mouthing the words and making signs with their hands. Without me. I stared out of the window, all the passing traffic a teary blur. I really did feel sick, and so shaky. I curled up, with my feet on the seat, and pulled my coat over me. Sparks of colour exploded under my closed eyelids and all the noise seemed to swirl jaggedly around me. Maybe if I tried hard enough I could imagine myself at home. Though my eyes were shut, I couldn't shut my ears. Too much noise, too much laughter.

I was very tired from my restless night, so, as I'd hoped, I fell into a light slumber. I was woken up by Ava, tugging on my arm. I hoped we were there, but I could still hear the buzz of the motorway. When I stepped off the heaving coach, I gulped in the fresh air, or as fresh as you get on the side of a motorway. We were at a service station. We all lined up in our tutor groups and were led by our tutors to smelly public toilets. I had no choice but to use one, but I pulled my T-shirt over my nose and didn't dare breathe in any germs. I used my sleeve to open the door. Then I washed my hands thoroughly. Most of the girls were reapplying thick layers of orangey foundation and eye stuff. I personally thought the dark eye make-up and orange skin made them look like Halloween pumpkins, but I just about had the wit not to say my thoughts out loud.

I suddenly felt a wave of self-consciousness, like I was seeing myself in the mirror for the first time. I saw a puny girl with a slightly spotty face, lanky limbs and thin black hair. I realised how...different I looked. I tried taking out my hair and doing that pouty face in the mirror. I heard a snigger and stopped, abruptly. It was like a sudden, vacuous light on who I really was; all the little things I had never had, like a boyfriend - not that any of the Year 9s were promising candidates. I watched Ava and Emily pose with their phones for a selfie, and then type. I quickly peered at my own phone. Instagram.

'So happy to be travelling with my bestie, @Emily_xo_Diva. Love you forever! You're so much fun slayy xx.'

My eyes stung with tears. *I* was her best friend. I know that sounds so petty and ridiculous. Even so, I told Ava this when we were back outside. She just shrugged.

"I don't get why you have to be so precious, Zoe. It's way more fun to have lots of friends. You'd like Emily really, she's so much fun!"

Why did that hurt so much?

Because you know the truth, Zoe. Why you have no friends.

Before we got back on the coach, Mr Macclesfield led us to some sickly looking grass at the side of the building to eat our lunch. I knew there was no way I could eat. I felt so scared. So shaky. So overwhelmed. So sick.

I went and sat with Ava and Emily, and some other girls. They were all sharing a packet of prawn cocktail crisps, each girl delving her hand deep into the greasy bag. I dreaded to think how many germs there were. They didn't offer me any crisps. This was all wrong. I started flapping my hands by my cheeks out of habit, as I do when I'm scared. I thought I was being subtle. Obviously not. Emily looked amused and started laughing.

"Zoe, you honestly look so pathetic! Like you're a bird trying to fly!"

She imitated me and Ava started cracking up. I clenched my fists behind my back.

"Please stop," I tried to say, but my words just fell to the straggly grass and sank under all the noise.

"Look, Zoe, we don't actually want you here. Go and sit with the other special bitches over there," said Emily, pointing to the group of pupils with learning difficulties who were sitting with a special educational needs and disabilities teacher.

I burned with the unfairness of her words. How derogatory those syllables were. How if you don't perfectly fit into the select 'upper crust' of society, they sneer you away and cast you off to rock bottom.

"Don't speak about them like that, Emily," I tried to say, tangled with injustice, but my words fell down, invisible beneath the noise.

Unheard. Forgotten. Unnoticed.

Chapter 4

Ellen

I hugged Mabel, even after the sound of her breathing had ceased; even though I strained to hear it, yet couldn't. Her arms and legs no longer flailed in exertion. Her small body lay lifeless in my arms. I wouldn't let them take her when the ambulance and police arrived. Mum was unconscious on the carpet. She wasn't moving either. I didn't know if she was alive or dead. I didn't really care. I just wanted Mabel back.

"I want her back!" I screamed to the ambulance woman.

"I know, sweetheart. Say goodbye and hand her to me," she said, her voice completely flat.

"No! Don't take her away!" I yelped, hugging her body to my chest.

"I know, darling, I know. But we need to see she's OK. Hand her over to me."

Was she thick?

Couldn't they see Mabel was quite clearly not OK?

I felt too weak and drained to keep protesting. I kissed Mabel on the top of her fluffy head. Her skin was so soft and tender. Her benevolent blue eyes looked up at me, through a milky glaze, as if to tell me not to worry and everything would be fine. I took her tiny, fisted hand, very carefully unwinding her perfect fingers, and put her hand in mine. I could still feel the warmth of her body under my touch. I buried my tears in her face one last time then handed Mabel over to the ambulancewoman, who passed her to a colleague. He examined her, looking grave, then shook his head, before handing her back. They both walked out of the room.

I knew Mabel was dead, but I wanted her back. I wanted to scream and cry, but I was the grown up. I had to help mum. I went over and tried to wake her up, shaking her shoulder in despair, but couldn't. I collapsed against her, sobbing that I was sorry for letting her down. A gentle police officer came over and sat beside me.

"It's OK, darling. You don't have to look after her any more. She's ours now," he said softly.

"What's your name then, sweetheart?"

"Ellen - Ellen Maclaren," I whispered.

"That's a pretty name," he said. "Do you think you could come with us now, Ellen?"

I looked desperately at mum. I didn't want to lose all of my family.

Then, suddenly, something snapped inside me. I broke like an elastic band, and all the anger exploded out of me like water breaking a dam.

"How could you do this to me, mum?!" I screamed, tearing and scratching at her body, and punching her face.

The police officer pulled me away, yelling and distraught, while two more paramedics strapped mum onto a stretcher and carried her outside.

"It's OK. We'll look after mummy," he told me gently. In the space of an hour, my family had been shattered. He sat with me until my breathing eased, and the emotions subsided.

"It's time to go now, darling," said the ambulancewoman. I wanted to ask what they'd done with Mabel, but I didn't quite want to know. The policewoman walked with me to my room to collect my few possessions. She looked shocked as she entered, and made notes. It made me feel so awkward. I felt ashamed. Why was I worrying about my room when my mum had passed out and my baby sister had died just minutes ago? My bed was some giant cushions mum had found at the flea market a while back. The market probably got its name because the cushions really did have fleas in them, as the first time I slept on them I woke up covered in bites. Mum had to sort it with some kind of powder. She'd covered the pillows in a sheet, and I had a discoloured duvet on top. I think a long time ago I had a proper bed and mattress, back when mum was well and we lived in a proper flat, but then she sold it to buy drugs. The bedroom walls were a sickly, damp ridden yellow, as though all the colour and happiness had been puked out. The windowsills were covered with mould that made me wheeze, and there was no carpet at all on the floors, just bare wooden floorboards. Draughts blew under the door and chilled me to the bone. I had a tiny, rickety table by my makeshift bed, on which I placed my best possessions: a kaleidoscope salvaged from a long-ago shopping trip, back on one of mum's good days; an empty rose-gold bottle of mum's old perfume with a pomander pump; and a tiny, shiny manicure compact mirror I had found outside on the pavement.

I looked around for anything I could take or really needed. In the end, I just grabbed the old cardigan I had for cold days and my three small trinkets, shoving them into an old rucksack. I realised I had nothing else.

"Come on, Ellen," the policewoman said softly.

"It's time to leave now. You don't have to worry any more."

On the way out, she peered into our fridge. There was half a bottle of milk, not fit to drink, an old knob of cheese that had gone hard and was smelly, and two cans of baked beans. There was nothing in the cupboards other than a couple of those cheap, instant noodle pots and mug soup. It was in that moment I realised for the first time how I had been treated all my late childhood.

I followed the policewoman out of the flat and down the stairs to the police car. The flashing lights scared made. It was all too real. There was an ambulance too, but the doors were shut. I wondered what was going on inside.

The seats in the police car were scratchy and it smelled of disinfectant and newness, along with sickly air fresheners.

All the while the policewoman was asking me all sorts of questions. She did it subtly, but the questions were niggling and personal. I slumped away from her, looking up at the galaxies of twinkling stars in the sky, wondering if Mabel was up there, looking down at me.

Chapter 5

Zoe

When we arrived, I rushed to get off the coach for fresh air and breathed in deeply. The air here smelled of forest and mud, and tasted of pine leaves, a nice comparison to the normal traffic and fast food. Maybe it wouldn't be so bad sleeping here. Maybe.

"Order, Year 9! Order!" Mr Macclesfield shouted as he glowered.

"Line up in your tutor groups and follow the instructors up to our camp, quietly!"

Two young men and a woman with her hair bleached purple at the tips stood by the huffing coach in muddy jumpers that said 'Ashwood Forest Residential' on the front, and 'Instructor' on the back. They also had lanyards round their necks with their photo and name, but I couldn't read them from where I was.

"Hello Cradisfield, and welcome to Ashwood Forest Residential Camp," said the lady.

She continued with a lot of stuff about how the place was founded, and what to do in an emergency. I didn't pay too much attention to this, as common sense told me that the river couldn't possibly overflow unless there was serious rainfall (which there hadn't been), so we wouldn't need the life jackets in the red cupboard.

I seem to have this habit of either listening when I don't want to, or not absorbing any information when I thought I was listening.

One of the young men told us to follow him and the other leaders up the path and not to overtake them. It had said on the email and letter to wear old clothes that we wouldn't mind getting muddy. However, Emily, nonchalant to this, was dressed in a weeny, strappy tank top that showed off her extremely flat stomach. (Well, to be honest, it showed off a bit more than that.) She was also wearing very tight ripped jeans the colour of white, with holey tights underneath. Most of the other girls wore similar outfits. Goodness knows why! Her shoes were also very strappy, with buckles and jewels. I couldn't help looking down at my own non-branded trainers, black leggings and childish loose T-shirt, and feeling stupid.

Emily sidled up to James in this outfit and wrapped her arm round him. Pathetic! I still don't understand all this stupid boyfriend, girlfriend nonsense.

I watched as they lagged behind the crocodile of tutor groups, Emily flirting like anything. James laughed and rolled his eyes, making a yawning motion. I spluttered.

The walk was long and muddy. I felt a secret joy at the brown splatters on Emily's white jeans.

Then, amongst some old gnarled oak trees, I saw the most exciting thing ever.

41

"Badger setts!" I said breathlessly to myself.

My arms tingled with excitement. At home, I had about five books on animals, with photos of their markings and homes. I'd always looked out desperately for any sign of wildlife, but no matter how endlessly my eyes strained, I'd never seen more than a sparrow pecking at rubbish amongst the traffic – oh, and a couple of times I had seen a scabby urban fox ruffling around the bins, and, inevitably, the London pigeons. There were always signs up saying 'Do not feed the pigeons', but I took little notice of them. I loved how they would coo around me, cocking their heads sideways to ask for more crumbs.

The excitement made me run up the side of the hill towards the twisted oaks. I crouched there, inspecting the holes, crusted with piles of earth.

Definitely badgers! Oh, how wonderful!

I'd always had an understanding towards animals much greater than towards people. They were so much simpler.

"ZOE BROWN, WHAT DO YOU THINK YOU ARE DOING?" came a loud, booming voice.

Oh, great! It was Mr Macclesfield charging towards me.

"DO YOU HAVE ANY IDEA HOW DANGEROUS THAT IS?" he bellowed.

I instinctively reeled at the noise and turned my back on him. He obviously thought I was being rude because as

I looked back, his face was flushed an ugly red. I hadn't realised that a crowd of people were staring up at me.

Oh, great! My plan of blending into the background wasn't working. Then I saw something that made my heart race. Emily and Ava crying...with laughter.

"COME DOWN, NOW!" shouted Mr Macclesfield, pointing one finger at me. His wrist was hairy and dark, and he wore one of those great silver watches that businessmen wear.

I worried it wasn't just me he'd scare.

"Shh," I said. "You'll frighten the badgers, Mr Macclesfield!"

I was being serious. OK, maybe I was being sarcastic, because, in a situation like this it is better to have your classmates laughing with you than at you. I had no respect for Mr Macclesfield, as he always had ways of humiliating me, and he didn't respect me, either. Peals of laughter came from below and I smirked. Mr Macclesfield was in anything but a laughing mood.

"Get. Down. Now." He said through gritted teeth. Each syllable pronounced and ominous, as the stubble on his beard stood out.

I reluctantly climbed down. Don't think I did it because of him. No. I did it for the badgers, because if I had stayed up there, Mr Macclesfield would have kept screaming, which would have scared the poor badgers silly. OK, maybe that's not the entire truth.

—

"You will walk with me," he told me, briskly. So, for the rest of the walk, I was humiliated with Mr Macclesfield as a partner. He smelled all too strongly of men's deodorant spray. He turned round to the instructor, who looked a little stunned by my outburst, and raised his eyebrows in an adult code way.

"I apologise. This one has issues," he said under his breath, glancing at me.

I was outraged. Issues? ISSUES? I did not have issues. I was just the same as anybody else! Wasn't I?

How dare he say that? Why was I different? I was exactly the same as any other teenage girl.

You know the truth, Zoe.

When we got to the camp, I was utterly exhausted from lugging my suitcase and night bag, but there was no respite. Two more instructors showed us to a smouldering firepit with logs. We all sat down. It was quite a squeeze. I looked for Ava and sat next to her, but Emily shoved me out of the way with her pointed hips. I felt so betrayed. Tears watered my eyes, but I knew it would be fatal to cry. No. Of course I wasn't going to cry. I didn't have 'issues' like Mr Macclesfield had said.

I couldn't concentrate properly when the instructor was going on about safety around the campfire. It was way too squashed and claustrophobic.

Stop giving yourself labels, Zoe. You're not claustrophobic.

I could feel hot breath on my neck.

No, don't think about it.

Luckily, the instructor finished his spiel and showed us around a poky kitchen with a crusty dining room attached. Both looked grubby. I imagined all the germs.

"Now to your cabins!" ordered the instructor. "Follow me!"

He led us along stony paths to an array of cabins; about eight small ones with bunk beds and six bigger ones, each with one bed. I was definitely sleeping on my own. The thought of all the rise and chatter of girls keeping me awake made me shudder. It wasn't just that, it would be the smell of make-up, cheap body spray, sweat and girl. No, I couldn't do that.

"Right, boys on the left, girls on the right. Each cabin sleeps eight, so please get into groups quickly and sort out your things, then in half an hour I want you all dressed in your swimming clothes for our first activity," announced Mr Macclesfield in his sombre voice.

I immediately ran over to one of the single cabins and let myself in. It wasn't too hot, with an adjustable heater. I tried out the mattress. It wasn't *too* bad, although it was quite hard. I pulled out my duvet and pillow and placed them on top with my old teddy, Mr Snuggles, and put mum's striped shirt under my pillow. The letter had specifically said 'a light sleeping bag' on the packing list, but I had told mum diffidently that the slippery, slidy feel of the sleeping bag was most definitely not comfy. I wasn't a vegetable and so I didn't need a bag.

I suddenly missed mum so much. Not just mum. It was all the little things of my house and routine. Home. I brought out mum's stripy T-shirt from under my pillow and nuzzled it, curled up on the bed, tears streaming down my face, when Mrs Rhys, another form tutor, walked in.

Her eyes practically popped out of her skull when she saw me on the bed.

"Zoe! Wha-what are you doing here?!" she asked.

"I'm setting up my cabin, Mrs Rhys," I croaked, hastily wiping my face.

"What? These are the teachers' cabins, Zoe! You'll be sleeping with your friends in one of the other cabins," she said.

No, no, no. This was all going horribly wrong.

"I...don't want to," I stammered

"Yes you do! It will be good fun! Now hop along!" she said, irritated by this point.

She flung my duvet and pillow carelessly into the carrier bag along with mum's T-shirt and Mr Snuggles. I'd had him since I could remember, hence the name. I knew I was way too old for a soft toy, but it hadn't stopped me from cramming him into my night bag.

"Why didn't you bring a sleeping bag?" Mrs Rhys huffed.

I didn't answer, looking down at my feet as I exited the cabin.

Ava was coming back from the toilets so I followed her back to her cabin. When I walked in, it was unbearably hot and crowded and smelled of girl, along with the overpowering smell of cheap body mist, like I had predicted. Emily sighed when she saw me, and Ava raised her eyebrows I think.

No, of course they wouldn't do that. Like mum said, they're your friends.

Five other girls bounced on bunk beds, with stuff flung higgledy-piggledy.

The only mattress left was one in the bottom corner with half a loose spring uncovered.

"There you go, Zoe," said Emily, smirking gleefully. "Maybe the badgers have been digging at it!"

Ava, Emily, Bella, Ivy, Charlotte, Nancy and Rebecca all cried with laughter. These girls were supposed to be my friends. How could I possibly sleep on a mattress like this? I'd at least assumed I'd be sharing a bunk with Ava. She'd said so, as she was supposed to be my best friend, but she was sharing with Emily.

"Ava, you said you'd be on my bunk," I stuttered, threatening tears again.

She just shrugged and sighed at me in a sophisticated manner.

"Honestly, Zoe, you are being difficult! Does it really matter?" she said. There was a pause.

"Do you want to work on our handshake?" I asked randomly, desperately trying to make things better.

At primary school and for the last couple of years, Ava and I had a special 'best friends forever' handshake routine to show our true friendship could never be broken.

Handshakes didn't have to be childish...did they?

I was desperate not to let go of the slipping rope of friendship we had left.

Ava looked mortified.

"Zoe! We're way too old for that now! That was like aaages ago."

"It was less than a year ago!" I said, but my words were invisible.

I was about to make my bed, neatly, when a voice called from out in the camp.

"I want you all dressed in eight minutes and not a second later!" bellowed an all-too-familiar voice.

The girls sighed and started undressing. I was shocked at how unbashful they were. They almost seemed proud to show off. Emily wore a tiny purple bikini (another thing the packing list had forbidden). It was, inevitably, even smaller than her strappy tank top. It clung to her, emphasising how effortlessly good looking she was. Even in the tight material of my costume I was thin and totally flat up and down. I felt too self-conscious, especially when Emily looked me up and down and smirked, aware of her own curvy body. Ava wore a tankini in ruby red, and she also looked very grown up.

The rest of the girls wore costumes, though none as babyish as mine. It was pale blue with dogs like Sally on. Emily just about had the guts not to say anything out loud. We filed out of the cabin. The startling daylight made me blink after the dark oak of the dorm.

Mr Smith led us back down the path, past the badger sett, then across the coach bay, and down another chalky path to a makeshift hut with lines of life jackets hung up in it.

"Right, line up in three rows and the instructors will fit you with a life jacket," ordered Mr Smith.

I watched in horror as the instructors touched and fitted each child. I closed my eyes and the fireworks started going off in my head. How could I cope with a stranger touching me?

Act normal.

Stop being different, Zoe.

Be just like everyone else.

When it was my turn, I went rigid with agitation. The instructor moved my arms around and tightened the straps around my waist and legs. I could barely move. It was squashing me!

"Please, it's too tight!" I breathed.

The instructor sighed deeply and slid his hand around the life jacket and straps.

"It's meant to be tight. It's the perfect fit," he said, irritated.

"It's too tight; I can't move," I sobbed.

The fireworks were getting louder and I could feel my pulse beating warningly.

"Look, *I'm* the instructor! I do this as my job and it is fine."

The life jacket got tighter. All the sounds echoed and rebounded in my ears.

Act normal, Zoe. Act normal.

I cried. I gasped. I wrapped my arms round myself and sobbed. Everything just felt too much. Too pressured. Too overwhelming. My mask had broken, and my scars were open and revealed.

"This is completely normal! Zoe's just having a tantrum," sighed Mr Macclesfield to the instructors.

NO. NO. NO. NO.

———

What was I doing?

I was being such a weirdo!

Ava will never want to be friends now!

Help. Help. Help.

The fireworks were still going off.

"Why is Zoe acting like such a baby?" sneered Emily.

"I'm so sorry about her, she really is difficult. Sometimes I wonder if I really want to be friends, but my mum says I have to be nice to her," muttered Ava - Ava, my best friend!

It was only a whisper, but I heard it.

No. Ava couldn't have said that. I was imagining things. She wouldn't do that.

Mrs Emmas (probably the nicest of the teachers) bent down next to me.

"It's OK, Zoe! Come on, we're going in the river now to kayak. Isn't that fun?"

She used that patronising tone you use for toddlers to get them to oblige you. I wanted to toss my head and tell her I was about to be 14, not four. I heard the crunch of gravel as pairs of feet trod on the chalky pebbles.

"I can't swim," I mumbled.

"You don't need to swim. You're in a boat, and anyway that's what the life jackets are for."

"It's too tight, and I don't want to do it," I muttered, defiantly.

"Look, why don't we follow the others so we don't fall behind, and then if you get there and really don't want to, we can sit and watch and take off the jacket, OK?"

I nodded, solemnly, and shakily stood up, then walked with Mrs Emmas to the river. The fireworks had eased and I could concentrate properly. The water looked so sparkling and spiritual, yet beautifully menacing. I suddenly wanted to be in its presence more than anything. Maybe it would ease my pain; calm me down.

The life jacket was still way too tight. I looked around to see if anyone was watching, and slowly, reluctantly, loosened the straps. There, so much better!

"Right!" said another instructor, putting on a falsely cheery tone, though I could tell she was tired from doing the same spiel all day to many different schools.

"Please get into groups of five and decide who will be head of the boat. Somebody who is reasonably strong, then three in the middle, and one person at the back."

"Quickly now," added Mr Macclesfield, trying to maintain dominance.

I saw Emily and Ava immediately run over to each other, embracing like they had been parted for years, then Emily sidled up to James and pulled on his arm. I saw him look apologetically at the gang of boys that were looking quite put out. Maybe Ava felt a bit bad, because she pleaded something to Emily and I heard a flicker of "Zoe" burning in their whispers. James looked awkward and stood to the side, giving me a matey wave. I heard Emily sigh, then they both came over.

"Come and be in our group, Zoe. You can be the tail end – no, the badger tail!" said Emily. She laughed, as did I. It was better to laugh with her than to be laughed at.

I didn't want to be stuck on a boat with virulent Emily, but I realised there was nobody else who I could vaguely say was in my friendship group. Another girl, Charlotte, also joined our group.

"As you are so strong, James, you should be the head," said Emily in her sickly tone, syrup practically oozing out of her mouth as she hung on to James' arm. I struggled not to laugh, then James caught my eye and made a vomit motion. Maybe things weren't so bad.

"Sure," he said, flatly.

"Why don't Ava, Zoe and Charlotte go in the middle and you go at the back of the kayak, Emily?" James suggested.

"No fear! Zoe can go at the end. With matchsticks like those for arms she'll hardly be able to lift the oar!" sneered Emily, her voice still syrup. I peered down at my arms, skinny and vapidly pale. James saw my expression.

"Emily! That is a horrid thing to say!"

53

Emily looked shocked, obviously not used to her 'boyfriend' going against her.

"It's just a joke!" she shrugged.

I didn't think it was a very funny one.

We all climbed into the rickety boats. The seats were hard and very damp. Little pools of brown water moved about eerily within it. The river may be beautiful, but I wasn't sure I wanted to be so near it now. I'd changed my mind, but it was too late. The boat was heading out into the river with the instructors and other kayaks.

"Keep up, Zoe!" hissed Charlotte. "You're rowing the wrong way!"

The wind suddenly picked up and I shivered. I couldn't wait to be back in the camp so I could be clean.

Wait!

How would I get clean?

There were showers, weren't there?

What if...? What if...?

I couldn't worry now.

"Right," said the instructor. "We're going to play some fun boat games! First, you are going to row your kayaks to those red buoys and back as fast as you can. Whoever gets back first is the winner!" he said, triumphantly.

"On your marks, get set, GO!" he bellowed, rivalling Mr Macclesfield's volume.

I rowed as fast as I could, but my arms ached.

"HURRY UP, ZOE," Emily kept bellowing from in front.

We still lost.

"Well done, everyone! That was really good," the instructor patronised.

"Now for our next game. One person from your kayak must stand up on the side of the boat. Whoever stands up the longest without falling in is the winner!"

Ava clamoured to do this one. The boat was so unsteady she lost her balance and splashed into the water almost straight away. Most of the others followed, after 10 or so seconds, but they just laughed, splashed and squealed then clambered back on. I was so, so regretting being there. I couldn't swim. I couldn't swim at all.

We played several more similar games, all ending with everyone falling in the water. Except me.

"Now for our last activity. This one is a bit like the first, except for an extra challenge – with your eyes shut!"

I was so glad this was nearly over.

"Zoe! You haven't had a go yet," said Emily in a sickly voice.

"Yeah, Zoe!" said Ava "Go on, you really owe us something after losing that race," she added.

"No," I said, weakly, "please!"

"Yes," said Emily, and pulled me up before I could stop her. I stood, hand outstretched, my eyes closed in fear. I couldn't fall in.

No! No! No!

The fireworks were sparking inside my lids again.

Not now, Zoe!

"On your marks, get set, GO!" yelled the instructor.

I tried to block out everything and concentrate.

Concentrate, concentrate, concentrate.

I felt a hand on my back. I felt a push. I felt my feet slip and I fell headfirst into the river.

I struggled to get to the surface, gasping for air, but I felt something hard holding me down.

Was I under the kayak?

Why wasn't the life jacket working?

Then I remembered how I had loosened the straps. I realised it must have come off when I hit the water.

Strangely, when I was underneath the water, I felt a sense of calmness. I liked it down there. I was alone. I had nothing to worry about. Detached from the pounding of my heart, the burning of my lungs and the whirlwind in my head. Everything was surreal. I felt free and accepted for the first time in my life. Alone. Trapped, and yet I was free.

I felt arms around me, pulling me up, then I was hurled on the boat as I coughed and spluttered back to reality.

Chapter 6

Ellen

When we got to the police station it was really late - or early, depending on how you look at it. The policewoman walked me through the doors. As soon as I stepped inside it seemed ominous. I was led into a cold, functional interrogation room, with a ceiling camera in the corner. I eyed it, warily.

"Sit down, Ellen, love," said the lady, pulling out one of the hard chairs from the interview table.

I was now close enough to read the name on the ID card on her uniform.

Sophie.

Beside her was a policeman with a notebook and pen. They both sat opposite me.

"Now, Ellen," started the man. "We need to have a chat with you. It is very important that you are completely honest."

"Don't look so worried," said Sophie.

"Will my mum get executed?" I whispered, with my eyes wide open.

"What? Of course not, sweetheart! Where did you get that idea from? We just need to get things straight," said Sophie.

"But my mum always said if I was a really bad girl, she would send me to the police to be executed," I whispered.

I hadn't realised I had said it aloud.

Sophie looked shocked and the policeman (Dave) took notes.

"Oh, Ellen. I can promise you that isn't going to happen."

"OK Ellen, do you have any other relatives; grandparents, aunts, uncles?"

I shook my head. It had always just been mum and me...and then Mabel. My eyes stung just thinking about her and I knuckled them quickly, knowing one tear would be fatal because I would never stop.

"You're absolutely certain you have no other blood relatives?"

"Certain," I stuttered.

After that, I managed to tell them I was 13 and confirmed my last name was Maclaren. I told them my address.

"What about school, Ellen?" asked Dave.

"I used to go to school when I was younger, but then mum said schools were a waste of time and didn't pay the bills, and that I would be far more useful working..."

Sophie cut across me. "Your mum sent you to work?"

I nodded.

"Where?"

"At The Fox and Horse."

She looked astounded, so I tried to reassure her.

"It's OK, I get home before 12. I can look after myself! It's mum's friend, Saul, who employs me at his pub. He pays me 10 quid an hour for bottling up and washing dirty glasses, and sometimes I help out behind the bar when it's busy. I can work the till, that's why my maths is good!"

Sophie looked really astounded now, though she tried to keep her facial expression hidden.

"Why do you look so worried?" I asked. "I'm just helping with the income like any other girl."

"Ellen, it's not right for girls of 13 to not attend school in order to be working, especially at a pub, sweetheart."

Dave took lots of notes, then talked in hushed tones into his crackly walkie-talkie. Sophie asked more questions, but clearly it was to relax me. What did I like to eat? What things did I like to do? I answered with limited responses. Then she went to a cupboard at the side of the room,

---

rummaged around and pulled out some pieces of lined paper and a bumper pack of felt tips which looked old and very dry.

"Can you show me how you spell your name, Ellen?" she asked. I guessed this was a ploy to see if I could write.

Well, I would show her.

I wrote: 'Ellen'.

I remembered how mum had taught me to write my name years ago when she was in a good mood. Mum had done lots of lovely things when she was in a good mood. But as the years went by, the good moods had become less frequent. One day, about two years ago, when the addiction was still brewing, she took me shopping to a big department store and bought me new pairs of jeans, T-shirts and jumpers, and then we had lunch in McDonald's. I remember that day, longingly. We were like any mum and daughter; happy and safe. But when we got home that evening, mum started on the drink again, draining one can after the other. She started shouting at me for dragging her out and wasting all of her money on clothes I didn't need.

"You are a spoilt girl, Ellen Davis," she had spat at me, and the next day she cut the clothes up with a pair of scissors and put them in the bin. Often, she would call me by my dad's last name, to show how worthless I was.

"Let's go into the office and sort things out."

Sophie led me out of the interview room, locking the door behind her. When we got to the police office, another

—

lady sitting behind a desk and a mountain of paperwork nodded at Sophie, seemingly triumphant about something.

"I've phoned the social and found emergency foster care for Ellen."

She smiled at me, then back at Sophie.

"It should all be sorted. We'll drive her round now. They say they can have her until we find a more permanent position."

In the car, Sophie tried to make happy conversation. There seemed nothing to be remotely happy about, for heaven's sake! I'd just seen my baby sister die and my mum was probably in some dank prison if she wasn't dead too.

Sophie said the foster parents were called Stephen and Naomi and were very nice. I didn't take much notice of much else after that; I was caught up in a hurricane of my past. However, as we were getting out of the car, I couldn't stop the urge to ask one more thing.

"Where's Mabel? Is she safe?"

"Who, Ellen?" asked Sophie.

"My baby sister. I think she might have died," I whispered, hating even to say the word.

"Oh…"

She looked awkward but also deeply sad.

"I'm sure the paramedics have taken care of things."

She didn't say any more, and I didn't have the will to ask.

The door opened before we even knocked and a plump lady, around her sixties, presumably Naomi, and a slightly thinner man in a dressing gown, probably Stephen, were there to greet me.

"Hello, Ellen!" Naomi beamed, like she'd known me forever.

I glared at her, feeling a knife of disloyalty through my heart. This woman wasn't my mum. I *had* a mum already. Maybe that's what made the tears roll down my cheeks.

"Come in, come in!" she sang cheerily, beckoning me. "Let me take your bag for you."

I knew she was probably trying to be kind, but I snatched the precious little I had left of myself away from her grasp, though maybe it didn't matter. I'd already lost the person I loved most in the world, forever.

"Leave off!" I cried to her face.

I wanted to hurt her because I was hurting so much, but she just stepped backwards, apologising.

"Of course. Sorry, Ellen."

Sophie followed us into the kitchen. She had obviously been here many times before, as she showed herself around with ease. The kitchen smelled of baked bread and fresh coffee. It felt...cosy. In the lounge there were several large sofas and children's play things in boxes stacked by the wall, and an electric fire with a guard. Naomi led me up the stairs and into a small, tiled bathroom. She started to run the taps, whilst having a tactful look in my belongings bag, when she thought I wasn't looking. She then went to a wooden cupboard. Rummaging around, she pulled out a super soft cotton nightdress, about my size. At home, I'd rarely had a proper bath, mostly because we never had any hot water, and the bathroom was black with mould anyway. Usually, I just washed my face and hands in the bathroom sink. Naomi added lots of nice smelling stuff that made white frothy bubbles on the surface of the water.

"Right, Ellen, you enjoy your bath. I'll be just outside the door if you need anything," she said cheerily in her singsong voice, closing the door behind her.

So, I tentatively peeled off my clothes and stepped into the water. Initially, the heat of the water was a shock, but as I gradually sank down into the silky water I relaxed. It felt so good to relax my throbbing muscles in steaming fresh water and to get properly clean. Naomi chatted away from outside whilst I sponged and rinsed my whole body with so many different soaps and gels. I smelled more luxurious than a perfume shop! She would prod me for answers if I didn't respond, probably as a ploy to make sure I hadn't drowned myself. Then, I reluctantly clambered out and dried myself with the snowy white towel Naomi had left for me, warm from the radiator, and pulled on my nightdress. Naomi was sitting adjacent to the door as I emerged, tapping away on her phone, but she smiled up at me.

"Was that a nice bath, Ellen?"

I shrugged, knowing this wasn't the sort of question that needed an answer.

Nothing in my life would be nice ever again, would it?

Stupid woman.

She wasn't my mum, I thought, angrily.

Naomi tactfully took in the many cuts and bruises that had become part of my damaged patchwork, and gave me a soothing cream to rub on the worst of them.

I was so tired, but realised I was also hungry. When had I last eaten?

Naomi led me through to a whitewashed room with a single bed, with a pale pink-and-white-flower duvet. When I slid my feet into the soft, silky bedding, finding a hot water bottle ready at my feet, and rested my head on the plump, squashy pillow, it felt like the most comfy place I'd ever been.

"Hang on a tick," said Naomi. "I'll be back in a minute."

I heard her bustle downstairs, and several minutes later she returned with a small tray. There was a very milky cocoa with a thick layer of froth on the rim. There was also a small steaming bowl of creamy fish pie.

"I thought you might need some hot food. I made the fish pie myself," Naomi said.

I ate gratefully, too tired and hungry to be angry at her for now. After all, it wasn't her fault. She was just doing her job and trying to be kind, I suppose. The fish pie was so soft and milky, and the chunks of fish so tender and light they just slid down.

"There now, Ellen," said Naomi. "Settle down to sleep now. Stephen's and my room is opposite. Just come in if you need anything."

There was a pause.

Then, I felt the wall of anger weaken.

"Thanks," I whispered, sleepily.

I'd never known what proper, tender care was before. But maybe, just maybe, I might find it here.

Chapter 7

Zoe

When I was on land, I still couldn't stop coughing.

I was given a long lecture about the dangers of my actions in the bullying, authoritative way adults do when they want you to be scared.

Well, I wasn't scared of them.

I knew I was scared of Emily, though.

They walked me slowly back to camp as my legs were so shaky. When we arrived, the instructor and Mrs Rhys swaddled me in scratchy towels and sat me by the fire. They kept asking if I was OK.

I was fine, wasn't I?

It was just a bit of water.

No, actually, it was way more scary, but that's the thing when something really scary happens. I try to make it out to be a joke and not a scary situation at all. There was, however, a small part of me that knew the darker truth. I had wanted to stay down there. It was so...peaceful.

They called a first-aider to come for some reason. He checked my temperature and kept asking me if I felt dizzy or faint. I kept saying I was fine, although I was shivering a lot. He did lots of silly tests, then finally left me alone. Worriedly, Mrs Rhys came over.

"Why did you volunteer to jump in if you weren't confident in the water, Zoe?"

For a moment, a very small part of me hoped I could tell her, then common sense and fear took over. I pictured Emily in my mind, and all the powerful things she could do. I tried to speak, but all the words got clogged in my throat. Instead, I looked at the mellow flames dancing in the light evening dusk.

"I think you'd better go and get some clothes or pyjamas on, Zoe," said the instructor.

"Please," I said, "Can't I have a shower first?"

I looked down at my skin, imagining all the germs crawling on it from school, the coach, the service station, Ashwood Forest and the river. I saw them wriggling around. I couldn't contaminate my clean clothes.

"What?" said the instructor.

"A wash," I responded.

"Oh, we normally have a rule. Showering is from 6-8, morning and evening only."

But then she looked at my painful expression.

"Perhaps I can make an exception, because of what happened today. No longer than 10 minutes, mind!"

"Thank you so much," I breathed.

Slowly and regretfully, I headed back to the cabin. I had to pick my way through tights, hairbrushes, make-up and bottles of spray to my bunk and suitcase. I couldn't bear to see everything so out of order. I unzipped my suitcase and took out my wash bag, towel, non-branded joggers and old hoodie. I nuzzled my head into the joggers and imagined Sally and her warm doggie tang, then I picked up mum's crumpled T-shirt and Mr Snuggles. I nuzzled them too. I wanted my mum. I just wanted home, but I had to try and be brave.

I walked down to the shower hut and let myself in. The shower floor was slimy with residue; it was damp and gritty. I grimaced then stepped into the shower. Thank goodness it was hot. I soaped up my face flannel, breathing in the comforting, clean smell of my mango body wash. Then I sloshed the flannel over my face, arms and legs, scrubbing at them. I then did my feet and hair. I still didn't feel clean. I timidly stepped on to the filthy floor and dried myself, then pulled on my joggers and hoodie and went to check out the toilet.

The toilets were worse than I had imagined. Ramshackle huts draped with heavy cobwebs. There was even a dead spider in the toilet. Poor thing! What a horrid way to die.

I went back to camp and sat by the burning fire and had some banter with James, which made me feel a lot better.

Friendships with boys are so much easier than with girls. Why is everything so complicated?

Then we heard footsteps. The others were coming back. James and I instantly stopped talking as Emily's shrill voice cut through the dusk.

"Oh, James, sweetie!" Emily said, still in her tiny bikini with a towel slung round her shoulders. She made sure it was positioned so as not to block any flesh. *SO* pathetic! She threw her arm round him. I noticed as James went stiff.

"Sorry you got so upset," she said, smirking at me. "Though it was a joke, Zoe."

"She was really scared, Emily. That was so mean back there," whispered James, to my surprise.

"I said it was a joke, wasn't it, Zoe? We talked about it in the cabin, how it would be funny to be pushed into the water, didn't we?"

I didn't answer.

Emily's face was menacing, though still falsely nice.

"Didn't we?"

Her voice remained pleasant, but with a strong edge that only I could hear.

I nodded, stiff with fear.

James looked slightly reproachfully at me. Emily looked satisfied, then got up to get changed into some clothes. She'd undone her bun to allow her long blonde hair to cascade down her sleek back.

I sighed.

Why couldn't I be perfect? Why wasn't I shapely? Why wasn't I beautiful? Why couldn't I just be normal?

"She's pathetic at times, but why didn't you say it was an arranged joke?" said James, once Emily was out of earshot.

He then shook his head.

"You girls! I just don't understand. If us boys fall out we just punch each other round the head, then they're your mate again and the matter is finished."

I laughed and continued our banter about James being a rebel because I had seen him chewing gum on the coach.

"Only naughty people chew gum," I laughed.

"So, everyone in the entire school is a rebel?" he joked.

"Shut up, rebel!" I said, and we both collapsed with laughter.

Maybe things weren't so bad.

Mr Macclesfield's voice boomed through the serene evening, making the group of sparrows on the grass fly off into the watery dusk.

"Year 9, tea is ready! Come and sit down in the dining room in your tutor groups and wait to be served. Absolutely no pushing or shoving!"

I reluctantly went and sat down next to Ava and Emily. I hated the noise of the massive, echoey room, filled with a cacophony dancing in the air. I could smell the most overwhelming stench of gravy and vegetables. I didn't like packet mash. It was too gritty. I only liked fresh vegetables cooked in the crispy way, not the essential frozen peas, sweetcorn and carrot chunks - the sort that dry out and smell of old-lady wee. And the idea of putting a dead animal in my mouth made me shudder. I decided I wouldn't eat. No way. So, when my tutor group was called up to be served, I stayed sitting where I was.

"Zoe Brown! Are you deaf?!" called Mr Macclesfield. "Food, now!"

No, I wasn't deaf.

Tears stung my eyes and I crumpled them so as not to let out any leakage.

Mustn't cry. Mustn't cry. Mustn't cry.

I put my fingers over my ears to block out the noise.

Deep breaths. You're doing great, Zoe!

"She's covering her ears, Mr Macclesfield," said Emily, her words as sweet as sugar, though I knew they were more likely to be poisonous.

"Well then, if Zoe is too ignorant she'll have to go without then, won't she?" he snarled back, grinning.

Emily smirked, and when she came to sit back down, she slyly pinched me hard on my wrist, her long, false nails embedding into my skin.

"Baby!" she hissed.

I couldn't stop the tears this time. I wanted James but he wasn't in my tutor group. I was stuck and trapped. I wanted mum and Sally. Whenever I was sad, all I wanted to do was to bury my wet face into Sally's soft, silky fur. She licked my cheeks with her wet, pink tongue, and thumped her tail. Her soft brown eyes would stare up at me, lovingly.

"Are you OK, Zoe?" came a voice.

It was Ava. I don't think she was really concerned. She was just trying to make up so it would look better in front of people.

"She's fine. Aren't you, Zoe?" said Emily, talking in the tone you use with toddlers, as she daintily cut up her sausage into bitesize pieces so as not to smudge her lipstick.

I nodded, not risking another pinch. I got a sharp kick under the table instead. I noticed Ava ate her food in the same way as Emily. Maybe she had put lipstick on too.

When everyone had finished their dinner, we all had to scrape our plates and put them in the big plastic dish which Mr Macclesfield filled with hot water.

"Now, I need somebody to wash up."

He peered around us, slyly.

"Zoe," he said, pointing at me ominously.

He must have seen my agonised face.

No way! I imagined all the knives and forks that had been in people's mouths, and all the germs and viruses, and peas and bits of sausage rippling about in the lurid water.

"Go on!" he said, and steered me to a little wooden work surface outside. Then he left me.

"The rest of you, half an hour by the campfire until dark at 10 and then go to bed. Not a sound! I want you all to be nice and spritely for a careers' workshop tomorrow!" ordered Mr Macclesfield.

"Off you go!"

I heard chattering and laughter. This was so unfair. I stood gagging at the putrid water, sobbing. Then I heard footsteps. It was James.

"It's OK, Zoe."

I sobbed, unable to speak.

"Look, I'll wash and you dry. Is that OK?"

I nodded, spluttering.

"You're...so...kind," I sobbed.

"It's nothing," he assured me.

We stood there for a few minutes, washing and drying in unison.

"Thank you so much," I whispered.

"You know, my brother's autistic, Zoe. I understand," said James. "I understand."

The words hit me in the face as if all the lurid water had been tipped over me. I stopped, heart beating, the trees collapsing in on me.

Autistic?!

WHAT THE HECK?!

I wasn't autistic.

Where on earth had he got that idea from?

I felt anger and hurt bubble and hiss in my stomach - the magma searching for a way to escape.

Tick. Tick. Tick.

I WASN'T AUTISTIC!

I WASN'T!

James saw my distress.

"Hey, I'm sorry! Are you OK?" he asked, and I shouted.

"NO, I'M NOT! HOW COULD YOU SAY SUCH A THING? I AM NOT AUTISTIC!"

I screamed at him, my mask gaped open, all the anger exploding in a hurricane, before I slapped his arm. Then I reeled back, shocked, before running off into the dusk.

Maybe I shouted because I was hurt? Because it was an insult? Because I was tired? But deep, deep inside, I knew the real reason why. And this was where my nightmares began.

"Bed, Year 9! Get changed those of you still in clothes, then get into your cabins. You know where we are, but don't disturb us unless it's an absolute emergency. Understand? Breakfast is at 7:45, so be sure to be up by then."

And that was it.

Anger and confusion still whirled round my head and my brain was on fire. How could I have said those things?

It was pitch black now, but there were small beacon lights dotted along the path, and I had my torch. I followed them, opened the door to the cabin, climbed up the ladder and got into bed, for once not bothering to brush my teeth.

I struggle to write what happened next in those endless, painful hours. I squashed my face under my pillow to stifle the sobs of utter homesickness and sadness. I wanted to go back in time and take back what I had said.

I don't know if Ava heard, or if anyone did for that matter. Nobody came to comfort me, or even ask if I was OK. They were all practising hairstyles and messing about in the eerie moonlit cabin with make-up caked on their faces, posing with their phones in the mirror, bums sticking out. It wasn't right. These weren't the sounds I was meant to hear when going to sleep. I was meant to hear the buzz of mum and dad, and the 10 o'clock news downstairs, and the gerbils digging, and Sally yawning.

"Mum," I whispered.

It came out as a melancholic croak and I snuffled into her T-shirt.

After a while, I began to hear sighing and snoring. After a longer while, even Emily's shrill whispers and giggles faded. Silence! At last!

I couldn't sleep.

I needed home.

I crept out of bed and followed the lit path to one of the teacher's cabins, and knocked.

I heard a groan and a muffled swear, then Mr Macclesfield opened the cabin door and sighed heavily.

"For goodness' sake, Zoe! This is the limit! It's past midnight! Go back to bed!" he grumbled.

"I need to go home," I begged hoarsely.

"Don't be ridiculous! You've caused enough trouble today as it is," he snarled, and slammed the door on my tear-stained face.

"You don't understand. It's not my fault," I whispered.

But then whose fault was it?

I sloped away, sobbing. I couldn't go back to bed. Not now.

I heard the distant lapping sound of water. It was so soothing. I remembered how mum used to play me water noises to help me sleep. I found myself creeping past the wooden huts of the toilets, over the little fence and out of the camp, even though this was strictly forbidden.

I didn't care.

I didn't care a bit.

I slipped easily down the long stone path in my slippers, past the badger sett and lifejacket hut, and past the coach bay. I went down the muddy path, until I stood before the river. The moon shone down on the water, reflecting its soothing light and bathing the scene in a milky warmth. I breathed in and sighed. I didn't feel calm, that would be a lie. However, I felt content and more peaceful. How could that same place bring so much emotion?

On the way back, my torch reflected off a black and white furry face. I stood rigid with excitement. The badger stared at me for a few seconds, in shock, then scuttled back up the muddy bank, and disappeared down into its sett, ready for a good night's sleep.

I can hardly bear to write what happened next.

I could sense something as soon as I crept back into the cabin. It was now dark, other than somebody's small nightlight in the corner. I climbed up to my bunk and pulled the covers over my head. I remember hearing smothered giggles and splutters from the bunks around me. I searched around for mum's T-shirt. It wasn't there. I sat up, my heart beating. I had left it under my pillow! I felt again, and drew out the familiar body of my teddy, and burst into fresh tears. Mr Snuggles was only a body. His head had been severed off, and I knew exactly who had done it!

Chapter 8

Ellen

As my eyes sleepily opened, I saw I was still in the whitewashed room. A streak of cool autumnal sun seeped through a small chink in the curtain, illuminating the room in a refreshing warm glow. I wanted to savour this moment. My whole being was still in a distressed torment, but I could feel a very faint bandage of safety around me. Faint, but certain. Just at that moment, my door creaked open, and I saw Naomi balancing a breakfast tray.

"Good morning, Ellen! Did you sleep well? I figured it might be easier for me to bring you some breakfast in bed instead of eating downstairs with us."

She placed the tray down on the floor so she could arrange the pillows at the head of my bed, so I was nicely propped up. Naomi then lifted the tray carefully on to the duvet.

I stared in astonishment.

Was this all for me?

On the tray there was a frosted glass of orange juice, alongside a mug of steaming milk, all frothy on the top. There was a creamy bowl of porridge with syrup on top, drizzled in the shape of a smiley face. In another smaller bowl was some sliced apple, alongside a plate with two pieces of hot buttered toast on it, with an accompanying jar of strawberry jam. Naomi had even gone to the trouble of picking some slightly sad-looking autumn flowers from the garden.

"Is this all for me?" I asked, uncertainly.

She laughed.

"Of course it's for you, Ellen! Don't worry if you can't manage it all though. Eat up now. You need some nourishment!" she said gently, tapping the weak twig of my arm.

I honestly tried to eat this lovely breakfast; however, after a couple of mouthfuls, I was uncomfortably full. Months of little food had caused my stomach to shrink.

"Done," I shrugged at her, still not willing to show any weakness.

Naomi half-smiled then took the tray away, apart from the little jug of wilting flowers which she arranged on my bedside table. Then she hesitated.

"I'll lend you some clothes for now. We have a lovely cupboard with different clothes in with all the children that spend some time with us here. Hang on a tick."

Naomi returned a minute later with a pair of jeans, a T-shirt and a pink hoodie. All looked a little bit washed out. She also produced fresh underwear, a vest and socks.

"I'll leave you to get dressed, then if you like we could go out to town and do a little shopping this afternoon, but only if you feel up to it, Ellen," she said, tactfully.

So, after I got dressed, I snuggled on the sofa and watched some TV in the morning, fascinated by all the channels. Then, Naomi and I went out in her car to the shops. Even with all the sorrow I was feeling in my life, it was still a sort of happy day. Naomi let me choose whatever clothes I needed and liked. The streets whizzed past in a blur, and for a bit, everything felt surreal, like this had always been my life.

In Primark, I chose a pretty velvet purple dress with a matching pair of tights that I liked. I looked at Naomi anxiously.

"Too much money?" I flustered.

Naomi smiled, warmly.

"Don't you worry, Ellen! Go and pick a couple more outfits."

So, I chose several T-shirts, three pairs of jeans with butterflies embroidered up the sides, and one skirt. Naomi then picked out two packs of underwear for me.

We then went into Marks and Spencer and Naomi helped me choose a decent coat. We then went for a snack in the M&S café. We both had a hot, buttered teacake and mug of tea. I only took a bite of mine, then circled my finger round the teacake to get the butter. I managed a feeble "thanks" as we walked out of the café.

"Don't you worry, Ellen. It's fine!"

Naomi, I had learned, was one of those people who was always cheery, but I could tell the sadness in her voice, which was sadness for me.

I'd borrowed a pair of too-big trainers for the shopping trip off Naomi. Mum didn't used to bother to get my feet measured most of the time, so throughout my childhood I had been trying to cram my poor toes into ill-fitting shoes. Even before the drugs started, she had always been slightly adjacent to reality.

Naomi took me into a shoe shop. The lady behind the counter told me to take my shoes off, so I did. 'Naomi's' bright white socks were stained crimson at the ends.

"Oh, Naomi, I'm sorry!" I stuttered, mortified, with tears trickling down my face.

Naomi looked shocked and sad, although she was calm as always.

"What's happened to your poor toes, Ellen?" she whispered.

I sat in silence, so upset that I had ruined the new white socks she had given me only this morning.

The borrowed trainers I was wearing were only a size or two too big. Naomi quickly glanced at the size and picked out two pairs of trainers and a pair of boots, then hurried us out of the shop.

We went back to her car and she propped my foot up on her knee whilst very gently peeling off the sock. My childhood of ill-fitting footwear had resulted in my toes becoming blistered and extremely sore. Naomi looked in horror at the many weeping sores on my feet. She saw how all my toes slanted, jaggedly and squashed, then she looked over my neglected body, with its patchwork of scars.

"I think we might go home now," she said, placing her hand on my shoulder. I didn't protest.

When we got home, Stephen looked very serious. He had his glasses on and was surrounded by paperwork and jottings. However, he smiled when he looked up and saw us.

"It's good news, Ellen," he said. "The social workers have found a local family who can foster you far more long term."

Chapter 9

Zoe

I flew into mum's arms as soon as I stepped off the coach.

"Hello, darling!" she said, hugging me. "Did you have fun?"

I glared at her.

Fun?!

For all she was my mum, she was being pretty stupid.

"What do you think?" I hissed, trying to hold back my tears.

"Zoe! Don't speak to me like that!" she said, trying to keep up with me.

"No!" I said, my anger rising.

"Zoe? What's the matter? Didn't you have a nice time?"

"NO! I didn't want to go, but you wouldn't listen!" I exploded at her, before immediately being flooded with guilt. "I'm sorry," I whispered, tears stinging my eyes.

"Let's have a chat in the car, Zoe," said mum calmly, taking my suitcase and putting it in the boot.

I quickly got into the car and let my emotions spill.

"Shh, shh," said mum, stroking my hair. "It's OK," she crooned whilst I sobbed. "What happened that was so bad, hey?"

I opened my mouth to tell her. To tell her about how nobody had wanted to sit by me on the coach. To tell her how Emily had pushed me into the river. To tell her how Mr Snuggles had been beheaded. To tell her how James had accused me of being 'autistic', and how mad I had got at him. I wanted to tell her. But I couldn't. I needed to stay friends with them, because if I didn't...who else would I have? If I told mum, I knew she would phone the school and report Emily, and maybe even Ava, for bullying. Or she would at least get upset and angry, and be straight on Messenger to Ava's mum in a polite way of 'Zoe's been feeling very left out and hurt, could Ava make a special effort to look out for her in future?', then the air would be tense and sad all evening. I needed them. I needed their friendship. So, I just shook my head.

"Let's get you home," said mum.

I knew I couldn't tell mum, but there was somebody I could tell.

As soon as I ran in the door, I went to Sally's dog basket. She lay there most of the day nowadays, apart from her small gambol to the park and back each day. I curled round her whilst she licked my face, gazing up at me with

---

her knowing brown eyes, telling me it was OK, thumping her tail, her grey face resting on my knee.

I suddenly felt utterly exhausted, after three sleepless nights, that I decided (after a thorough shower) to go straight to bed. So, I picked myself up and tried to compose myself.

It's OK, Zoe! You're safe now!

Except I wasn't. I felt the buzz of my phone in my pocket and peered at the notification centre. It wasn't any of my contacts.

'Heyy F-R-E-A-K,

So you've been hiding all this time? Well you can't hide any more (: '

What did that mean?

I had a horrible knot in my stomach.

I felt another vibration as a photo was sent through. It was a screenshot of another chat. The top read 'James' with a silly emoji heart and ring. She had scribbled out everything else, bar one message.

'Emily, Zoe's autistic!'

I felt the room spin around me, and the fury rise. The fireworks exploded behind my eyelids. Little did I know this was only the start of my problems. I pressed 'caps lock' on my phone and the fury exploded into words. I sent the message.

I could hear them before I saw them. Then I could feel them; the soggy chips over my head, the water sprayed at me, the side-eyes, and the cruel comments.

"You're a freak, you know that?"

"She's a special bitch."

"I had to partner up with the freak for PE today because my friend was away. Can you imagine?!"

Freak. Freak. Freak.

Then one day they started on my bag. Emily was much taller than me, and she held it high in the air, laughing whilst all my belongings fell on to the floor and I scrambled desperately to retrieve them.

Mustn't cry. Mustn't cry. Don't cry.

It wasn't just my bag; it was my belongings inside my bag.

She helped me pick them up afterwards, so maybe it really was all just a joke.

It had been a fortnight since the residential; the teasing and tension building up ever since.

I mustn't tell. I mustn't tell. I mustn't tell.

I was too scared.

The teachers were worried, but I couldn't tell. Nobody would get it. Nobody understood how every day there was a compulsive demon clawing at my brain, and it took every distraction to keep it at bay.

I remember with regret the way I had screamed with rage at James at the residential.

Why had it upset me so much?

I could pretend anything I liked, but deep down, I knew why. There was a niggling voice persistently at the back of my head.

You only got angry because you know it's true.

You know it's true.

When I'd walked into school on Monday morning, a few of the girls were whispering and pointing. I looked behind me, thinking it was something else. This made them laugh. But it didn't bother me too much because it was only a few of the popular, cool girls, and it was nothing out of the ordinary.

One break time, I went to my friend group's usual hangout spot to discover it was empty. I was confused as we had met here every break time for the past year. I wandered around all break time, looking for them. I couldn't find them at lunch either, or the rest of that week. When I caught Ava at the end of a lesson and asked where they all were, she gave a side-eye to Emily, who sighed and explained they now hung around the PE shed.

I went there the following break time, munching on an apple. The atmosphere fell dead as soon as I walked into the gang. I could feel a thousand unspoken insults hanging in the air. I stuck it out for the whole break, trying so hard to make the right conversation, but always seemed to say the wrong thing. Although no actual hurtful words were exchanged, I could just feel from the glances and exclusive talk that I wasn't welcome. So, most break times I went to the library to read or draw.

Words had never seemed to hurt me before, but now that one chanted word stayed in my head.

FREAK. FREAK. FREAK.

"So, you're autistic are you, Zoe?" snarled Emily, with her eyebrows raised and lips curling.

"No, I'm not! Shut your stupid face! Who told you that?" I protested, despite already knowing who had sent the messages.

Why would he spread such horrid lies about me?

Emily looked so tall in her rolled-up school skirt. She would later corner me in the corridor after school.

"Well, Freak, here we are again."

I looked around for Ava, but she was nowhere to be seen. Emily could see straight through me.

"Looking for Ava, are you?" she snarled. "What makes you think she would want to be friends with a sad, autistic bitch like you?"

She circled me, like a tiger stalking its prey.

"B-b-because she's my best friend," I stammered.

"Oh no she's not; not after what I've told her!"

Emily brought out her phone, showing me Ava's chat. She had sent a screenshot of the angry messages I had sent her the night I got back.

Shit!

I could hardly bear to read the response.

'OMG, Emily! That is so nasty of her. What a bitch! I am so sorry, bestie xxx.'

I felt a flare of anger inside me; a ball of fire that burned my stomach.

"Yes, Zoe, you freak!"

"I know, let's wash off some of that 'autism' of yours," she spluttered.

"I'm NOT autistic! Autistic people are sad, nerdy losers who have no friends."

"And what makes you think you aren't that, Zoe?"

"Piss off, Emily," I stuttered, trying to sound tough whilst making a run for it, but she grabbed my arm, wrenching it.

She then delved into her schoolbag and brought out a plastic bottle. I tried to run away, but she grabbed my shirt collar.

If I couldn't take flight, I had to fight!

At first, the liquid felt like an icy gush over my face, but then it burned and stung my cheeks with a horrid, harsh smell of chemicals.

I had to bite my lip to stop myself.

I mustn't cry. I mustn't tell.

Emily laughed uproariously.

"Doesn't the freak like white spirit?!"

"Ava!" I croaked; the ball of fire getting bigger.

"Ava isn't here, and she never will be. Nobody likes you, Zoe. Nobody at all, because you're a freak! Admit it!"

I trembled and burned, my face stinging. She drew her head close to mine.

"Admit it!"

I swallowed.

"I'm a freak," I whispered.

"And I bet your parents think that as well. You were born a mistake, Zoe Brown. A great big freak."

Freak. Freak.

"Why don't you go and kill yourself? Nobody would care, because you're a freak and a loser!"

Freak. Freak. Freak.

The ball of fire exploded inside me. I subtly reached for my fun water bottle and threw the contents over Emily. She finally let go of me. She was shocked, and her hair and shirt were soaking. I ran for it. I ran as fast as I could to the water fountain to splash and wash the white spirit from my face. I then ran for the school gates.

'You're a freak.'

The words echoed around my head as I ran across pavements and tarmac. Everything was a blur. Disconnected. I heard a screech of breaks and an angry beeping, and realised I had stepped on to the road. Apologising to the driver, I made a further bolt, heading for the park.

Freak. Freak. Freak.

Chapter 10

Zoe

I ran.

I didn't go home straight away. I went to my place.

My eyes were streaming; my heart was banging.

We had no garden at home, but on the way home there was a park. A large space of green...a proper park. Off to the side there were lots of bushes. What made it special was that it wasn't in an obvious place.

I crawled through the bushes, still crying, not caring if I ripped my blazer. Then I ran through the long grass to the cluster of trees and sat there. The leaves were so beautiful at this time of year, all different shades of amber, crimson, saffron and brown. I knew the leaves were dying. The ground around me was covered with crackling leaves, colourful and crisp like the trees above me, whilst the decayed brown ones lay silently underneath, ready to rot into the mud.

I sat there for a good 10 minutes, calming my aching head before stumbling back home, sobbing. When I got to our block of flats, I opened the door with the key I kept in my schoolbag. My hands were sweaty and shaking so it took several attempts. When the door finally opened, I was prepared to retreat to my bedroom, under the duvet with Sally, and the gerbils next door, to forget about today.

However, mum and dad were waiting, looking very solemn and nervous. Why weren't they at work?

"Ah, Zoe!" said dad, giving me a hug.

I went stiff because I hated the feel of his scratchy jumper on my face.

He used the tone adults always use when they want to tell you something they know you won't like, but hope, like anything, you'll go with it.

Mum and dad were giving each other looks and smiling awkwardly. I knew this was big.

Then dad sniffed.

"What's that smell?" he asked, puzzled.

I knew he was referring to the white spirit.

"It smells like paint remover..."

I had tried to wash more of it off my face and arms using the outside tap on our block of flats, and had stuffed my blazer in my schoolbag, but I knew I must still reek.

"I had D.T today and I was washing up and spilled the paint remover all over myself!" I said, hurriedly.

Dad didn't look at all convinced, but he let it go.

"Come and sit down, Zoe," said mum, putting on the kettle and arranging party ring biscuits on a plate.

She knew I couldn't stand hot drinks, so the tea must've been for her and dad. Instead, she poured me a cool glass of apple juice, with the usual ice cube I always requested. It felt so cool in my hot, guilty hands.

Mum and dad sat down with me at the table, looking at each other nervously.

"How was school, Zoe?" dad started.

I felt my cheeks burn and I looked down at the wood of the table.

"Fine!" I mumbled.

My face still stung a bit from the white spirit, but I daren't acknowledge it.

"We have some big news, Zoe," said mum. "We have been thinking about this for a while, but now it's definite."

My heart was beating faster. This was either going to be a dream or a nightmare.

"You know how you've always said how you would like a sister?" said dad.

I looked, alarmed, at mum's stomach. It seemed pretty normal, though with the usual mum plumpness.

"Are you...pregnant, mum?" I stammered.

Despite the solemn atmosphere, mum burst out laughing.

"Oh blimey! I hope not!" she laughed. "I'm 49, Zoe!"

My heart started beating even faster and my hands grew sweaty. I hoped I was wrong.

"We would like to foster, Zoe," said dad. "We have thought about it for several years and have been through lots of rigorous checks and tests. They passed us a few months ago and..."

My head buzzed and I felt sick. They couldn't foster! I couldn't imagine having to live and cope with another person in the house. What if she touched my things? What if she hurt Sally or the gerbils? What if she steals mum and dad for herself?

"We have been asked to foster a girl," said mum.

"Her name is Ellen and she's 13...the same school year as you! I am sure you will get along really well once she settles...and she's had a really hard time. We really think you would be so good at helping her settle."

I knew they were trying to flatter me, to get me on side. Well, it wasn't going to work.

"We have arranged to meet her on Saturday," said dad. "And then, if everything goes to plan, and the social workers and Ellen are happy, we will arrange more meetings, and then Ellen will come and stay with us."

Everything was too much. The ball of fire returned, more blazing than ever.

"Well, this is my home, not some Ellen's home! And I am not sharing my space or my room! They're mine! And have you ever thought about how many germs she has? I bet she's a nasty, bratty teenager and if you foster her, I will never love you again!" I exploded, before running out of the room, out of the door and down to my special place, where nobody could find me.

Chapter 11

Ellen

It was all arranged. Naomi and I went to have a meeting with my social worker, Helen, and she showed me pictures of my new family. Their faces looked so warm and friendly, and so very...soft. These were feelings I had never had in a family of my own.

Amy, my new foster 'mum', had soft brown hair in a loose bun, secured with a pink scrunchy. Tim, my foster 'dad', had grey hair, and it was rather thin. However, the thing they had in common was their beaming smiles.

Zoe, my foster 'sister', puzzled me. She smiled in all the photos, but only with her lips. Her eyes always remained sad and deep. Zoe had long, wispy black hair in two messy plaits down her back. She was also quite short for her age. We were a world apart.

My new family had also sent a video, with each person talking a bit about themselves. I fizzed all over with excitement when I watched it, but there was a part of me that felt deeply disloyal to my own mum and sister, Mabel. I watched, transfixed with emotion.

"Hello, Ellen!" said Amy, warmly.

"We are so excited to meet you on Saturday," added Tim.

They were all sat on a big sofa, with Zoe in the middle.

Zoe looked so sad and never looked at the camera. I couldn't understand why. She had everything...an education, food, loving parents. All things she probably took for granted.

"Yes," whispered Zoe on the video. "I can't wait to meet you, Ellen," she said, flatly.

They talked about their favourite hobbies. I discovered that Tim liked bike riding and the piano, and he also played the cello. I liked the sound of that instrument. Amy liked baking and reading, and Zoe liked dogs, gerbils and art.

After we watched the video, Helen told me something about Zoe.

"You see, Zoe finds new situations hard."

"She might be a little tricky to get to know to start with," added Helen. "Zoe sometimes gets very anxious about things."

"But I know she will grow to enjoy having someone of the same age around," added Naomi quickly, seeing my agonised face.

There was still something I needed to know. A burning question that had been sat in the pit of my stomach for the last fortnight; the answer to which would be painful.

"Mum?" I whispered to the room.

Helen gave a sideways look to Naomi, who nodded.

"I'm going to be frank with you now, Ellen. Is that OK?"

I nodded.

"Your mum had suffered a drug overdose and was in a bad way. She was in hospital all last week. She's now in temporary holding until court, which should be in around seven or eight months, given the severity of the situation."

"Can I see her?" I asked.

"I'm so sorry, Ellen. You won't be able to see your mum until after court."

"But I want my mum!"

I broke down, sobs burning my throat.

For all the times I had tried to be strong, I wanted the person I loved most in the world to hold me - not some strange people doing their job. I couldn't get over how things were moving so quickly. Scarcely a fortnight ago I was at home. Now I was an abandoned parcel everybody kept passing on.

"I know love, I know," said Helen, her voice heavy with sadness, handing me a box of tissues.

"We're only doing this to keep you safe, Ellen. We will all try and make things the best for you as we can."

"And what about Mabel?"

Helen looked blank.

"My baby sister. She died and they took her away," I said, matter-of-factly.

"I was going to bring that up with you, Ellen. She is currently being held locally at the mortuary. What would you like to do as a goodbye to Mabel?"

"Can we bury her in a church?" I asked.

I had never been religious, but I liked the thought of something that was clean and peaceful, so she could sleep in happiness.

"I will have a look at the options and we can discuss it at our meeting on Monday. We have also arranged some sessions for you to be able to chat, once a week, to a lovely lady about any worries or feelings, for as long as you need."

She looked at her watch and stood up, as if reciting off a script.

"Take care, Ellen."

Naomi also stood up, and thanked Helen. I scowled at her through a blur of emotion and ran out of the door. I didn't speak all the way back, and as soon as the car drew up, I ran up to bed, pulled the covers up and tried to escape reality.

On Saturday morning, I woke with a knot in my stomach. I had struggled to sleep, cuddling my new brown teddy. Naomi had bought him for me as a little gift; a gift that made me cry with joy and pain. I had a cuddly toy when I was younger. It was a bedraggled pink bear, fading, balding and worn at the ears as I used to suck them for comfort on those long nights mum would leave me alone, having had nothing to eat or drink for hours. Pink bear was my only friend, and I took her everywhere with me. I loved her so much and cared for her tenderly, the way mum never had for me.

Then, one terrible evening, pink bear was gone.

Mum was in a bad way, screaming for me to get her more drink, and she ended up retching on the carpet. I tucked pink bear into my armpit, stroking her ears so she didn't have to hear mum shouting.

I was only about eight or nine, and my hands trembled with fear as I fumbled with the vodka. The bottle had smashed on the floor, sending little shards of glass everywhere. Mum was furious. She crawled over to me, her eyes hazy and somewhat crazed, and started hitting out at me with shards of glass in her hands. They cut deep into my skin - I still have the scars. It hurt so much, but I had to be brave. I was the adult.

I had hugged pink bear whilst it was happening, letting my tears be absorbed into her fur. I saw her glass eyes for one last time before mum snatched her off me and cut her head off with the big kitchen scissors.

She didn't stop there. She cut pink bear up until there were only little bits of faded pink felt and stuffing on the floor. I recall sobbing in deep despair.

"Serves you right, you disgusting, lazy and stupid girl! You are your father's child!"

Stupid. Lazy. Disgusting.

The room seemed to spin around me.

Stupid. Lazy. Disgusting.

I could feel the blood trickling down my back. I could hear mum's voice bellowing deep inside my head. I was screaming now, trying to get the images out of my head.

Upon hearing the door open I screamed so loudly, I tumbled right out of bed, terrified. I thought it was mum coming for me with the broken vodka bottle.

"HELP! DON'T MUM, PLEASE. HELP!" I gasped breathlessly, my face blue, before fainting on the carpet.

I could still hear mum shouting as the room spun around me.

The room then gradually returned to stillness. All the time, Naomi was rocking me and muttering: "Shh, it's OK, darling! You're safe, Ellen."

"Mum..." I whispered, pointing around the room.

Naomi shook her head, sadly.

"No, Ellen, don't worry. We can talk more later...if you feel up to it. Do you still feel up to meeting your new foster family, because we can always postpone it, chickie?"

"Can't I just stay here, forever?"

Naomi looked deeply sad. "I wish I could do that for you Ellen, but this is only temporary accommodation."

I felt angry that nobody wanted me, and thought, if for no other reason, I would meet them out of spite. So, with Naomi's help, I shakily stood up. She helped me down the stairs and made me a small bowl of porridge, with cinnamon, along with sliced banana and a dash of cream and brown sugar.

"This should slip down easily, Ellen," she said, softly.

"Ta," I said, shakily, before eating.

I felt a lot better now.

At 12 o'clock, Naomi drove me to Pizza Express. All the way there I was terrified, and, a small part of me was extremely cross and angry. Angry with myself for being disloyal to mum...and angry with myself for not saving Mabel.

I looked out of the window, up at the sky. It was a crisp, late-September day, the sky so thick with white clouds the whole landscape looked untainted.

When we arrived, Naomi messaged Amy, my new foster mum, to make sure they were there. She then smiled and said we were going in to meet them. As I walked through the door there was a stale smell of sweat, cheese and bread, along with an undertone of tomato and fries. I was trying to concentrate on the smell rather than my emotions.

Everything was too much.

Too much. Too fast.

"Ellen?" Naomi said, softly.

I jerked and slid open my eyes, and there in front of me were Amy, Tim and Zoe.

Amy beamed at me and Tim was smiling so much I thought the corners of his lips might be torn in two from the strain. Zoe was the only one not smiling. She was scowling, but I remembered what Naomi had said, so I made a special effort, giving her a great smile. It gave me something positive to focus on.

"It's too crowded in here!" she snapped.

"It's all your fault, mum! Make the people stop being so noisy!"

Amy was still smiling, but her eyes darkened in Zoe's direction, and she said, through a gritted smile: "DON'T, Zoe! You're only embarrassing yourself."

Then she turned back to me.

"Hello, Ellen! It's so lovely to meet you in person."

"Hello, Ellen!" said Tim. "I can't wait to hear all about you!"

They turned to Zoe.

"Hi, Ellen," she said, not making eye contact. "This is so lovely," she said, expressionlessly.

"Hi," I returned.

"Well, let's go and sit down," said Amy.

She went up to the counter to be seated, but Zoe looked preoccupied.

"Mum, you promised!" she said, her eyes filling with tears. "You promised!"

"Oh, Zoe, please don't embarrass me," said Amy, wearily.

"NO! You promised you would email them so we could have the window seat!" Zoe gasped, internally.

I was shocked that Zoe could act like such a brat and treat her mum this way. She was lucky, but so carelessly nonchalant to the fact she had everything I had ever dreamed of. We may be the same age, but our maturity seemed distant.

"Mum! Get those people to move, now!"

"Zoe!"

Amy smiled apologetically at me. I glared at both of them. Why was Zoe crying over a table? Honestly! She really needed to chill a bit.

As the waiter showed us to a corner table in the busy room, Zoe scowled at him through sobby jerks. When we were all sat down, Tim handed out the menus.

"Well, Ellen, what's your favourite pizza?" he asked.

Was he crazy? As if mum would have ever bought me pizza!

Actually, I remember when I was little, before all the bad days, mum and I used to have oven pizza on a Friday, but when I ate it, I often discovered it was still frozen in the middle. I recall when I was a bit older seeing an advertisement for takeaway pizza in a shop window. It looked so nice my mouth watered! At the time, the troubles were brewing, and I hadn't eaten properly for days, so that night, when mum was at the pub, I rummaged around our bare kitchen. I was probably only about nine at the time. I fished around in the bread packet and found a crust. It was so mouldy it wasn't identifiable as bread. Mum often gave me mouldy food. I never knew what mould was, and if it was bad for you. I was often sick because of it!

When I'd got the bread out, I spread it with some ketchup and a knob of old cheese. I felt so ill after I had eaten it, and I couldn't make it to the bathroom in time. I threw up on the kitchen floor! I remember the sheer panic and terror of what mum would do when she came back. I tried desperately to clear it up, but then the door opened.

Mum was drunk again and staggered across to me. I sobbed as she saw the vomit.

"YOU DISGUSTING, LAZY GIRL!" she screamed right in my face. "You sicken me!" she snarled.

I sobbed that I was sorry, but there was nothing I could say or do.

Mum shoved my face hard down into the sick. I still remember the unbearable stench of vomit all over me.

No! I suddenly thought to myself. *I wasn't going to think about mum!*

I buried my face in the menu, not wanting anyone to see my tears, so I just shrugged at the favourite-pizza question.

A lot of the menu made no sense to me anyway, as I couldn't read very well. Even when I had gone to school, I had struggled with reading.

Naomi tactfully helped me.

"Here, Ellen, you can choose a small or medium size and add toppings of your choice. How about a margherita? That's just cheese and tomato. You can get a side of fries or salad. The soft drinks are here; see, they have juice...or Coke."

I nodded and pointed to what I wanted, but I still had a niggling worry inside me.

"This won't all cost too much will it?" I asked.

"Don't you worry, Ellen," said Tim.

After we had all ordered our pizzas there was an awkward 10 minutes when Tim and Amy tried to make conversation with me.

What were my favourite hobbies and subjects?

The questions soon petered out to lame ones, like asking about my favourite colour and animal.

I answered the best I could, but the foundation of my childhood was so poor I had nothing to base my answers on. I had barely been outside the barbed wire of my life, let alone to school for the last couple of years.

I then heard a buzz of a phone.

I was sitting next to Naomi and on the other side of her was Zoe.

I saw Zoe furtively look at the notification centre of her phone under the cover of the table. I couldn't help but peer over, as Naomi was deep in conversation with Amy about the secrets of a good shortcrust pastry. It was an unlogged number. A text. I watched Zoe's face as she read the five words.

'I will get you, freak!'

"Please can I go to the bathroom?" she muttered.

"Me too!" I said, hurriedly, after Zoe had got up and was out of earshot, desperate to find out what that message was about.

I followed her along the corridor to a public WC and crept inside a good 10 seconds after she did, not wanting her to know I was listening. She was in a cubicle at the end, and she seemed to be talking to somebody. Her voice was hushed and fearful, but I strained to hear.

"Please, I said I was sorry!" Her voice sounded panicky.

I silently slid into the cubicle next door and pressed my ear against the side, straining to hear the person on the other end of the phone. It worked.

"You are really going to pay for this, Zoe!"

It was a girl's voice, so unlike Zoe's. It was icy and menacing.

"You were the one pinning me down. What else was I supposed to do? Get a life! It was only water, you bitch."

"Oh yeah? And how can you prove any of that? I think you'll find it's you who's the bitch, Zoe!"

"Ava will believe me."

"You sure about that, freak? Or do you need me to remind you of the messages she's been sending me? You know I can tell at any time about what you did to me that day; it was literally assault. And it's all your fault! I don't blame Ava. I mean, it was an obvious choice."

"It was freaking WATER, Emily!"

I heard the sound as Zoe hung up, and then the ring as she phoned somebody else.

"Ava?"

"Huh, what is it now, Zoe?"

"You are still my friend, aren't you?"

"Yeah, yeah; whatever."

There was a pause.

Then Zoe asked as casually as she could: "What are you doing for your birthday this year?"

Another pause. Much longer.

"Oh...well, nothing really to be honest."

I heard a shuffle on the other end of the phone and a fainter voice.

"Ava, hey, who are you on the phone to now? I got the snacks."

It was a boy's voice this time.

"James...?" Zoe whispered, huskily.

"Oh, nobody! Just one of those scam calls," Ava said, and the phone was hung up.

I waited for Zoe outside her cubicle.

"Zoe..." I started, in shock and confusion.

"Ellen!" she gasped. Then her face darkened and she looked me straight in the eyes for the first time, though I could see what a struggle it was.

"Ellen, if you heard any of that...then I'm warning you! Don't tell anyone!" she insisted, her hand gripping my forearm.

I shook my head worriedly.

Zoe's eyes filled with tears.

"I don't want you in my house, Ellen. They are my parents, not yours, and if you dare mention anything you just heard there will be trouble. You don't get it, and you never will. Nobody will. So please, just stay out of it," said Zoe before she walked out.

On Tuesday, I had another meeting with Helen. She had found different options for Mabel's funeral. I said I hated the thought of her tiny body being burnt in fire.

"I want her buried in one of them coffin things with a blanket and teddy inside so she knows she is never alone."

"Of course, Ellen. I will tell the undertakers that."

"And can she have a stone angel to watch over her?"

"I'm afraid your mother's savings won't cover that, Ellen, but how about a small headstone, and we could ask for angels to be carved into the corners?"

"OK," I whispered, my throat throbbing with the effort to hold the emotion in.

"The burial won't be until after the court, which is due to happen around the middle of December, given the severity of your circumstance."

"Why is it taking so long?" I asked.

"That's actually pretty soon compared to most court cases. I understand this may be hard, Ellen, but by law you will need to be at the hearing."

"What?" I stuttered, though I knew what she meant, and I closed my eyes whilst the past flashed by.

"There will be lots of measures in place to make the time as comfortable as possible. You probably won't have to be in the room, it will most likely be on a live stream, and I will be with you."

I couldn't concentrate. I felt my cheeks grow hot, my eyes throb and my head spin. I got up to walk out of the room, and suddenly my legs went numb and gave way. I was falling, falling, falling...

When I woke, I found my legs propped up on a chair and Naomi squeezing my hand.

"Are you OK, Ellen? I think you just fainted with the shock of it all," said Helen.

They both propped me up slowly and Naomi helped me sip a glass of water. They made easy talk with me for a few minutes, until they agreed to call it a day.

Naomi helped me to the car.

It was pouring with rain and I was soaked through by the time we made it to the end of the road. We sat in silence in the car for a minute or so, then Naomi said gently: "I can't imagine the emotional strain you must be going through, Ellen. Please say if there is anything I can do for you. Your first session to chat things over starts in a few days. I so hope you can start to talk, as this will help you."

I stared vacantly out of the window, because nothing could help.

Chapter 12

Ellen

That night I woke up in a fever of adrenaline, convinced I was back at home. I could see mum, advancing towards me, her arms outstretched. I went to hug her, feeling the warmth and love of her body against mine.

Love.

Hate.

But then she grasped my head and started to shake it back and forth; my neck wrenching and snapping as the joints gave way. I screamed as she chased me, with her hands outstretched.

Then I felt more hands, but these ones were strong and plump; the palms soft from rose hand cream.

"Ellen, Ellen, it's OK. I've got you. You're safe!"

But I wasn't safe. Mum was in the room and she was coming to get me.

"MUM!" I screamed. "Don't let her get me!"

"You're safe, Ellen. There is nobody here, I promise."

When I opened my eyes, I saw mum had vanished, and a plump lady in soft cotton pyjamas had her arms round me.

"Naomi," I breathed.

I kept having hallucinations like this for the next few days, though not as severe.

On Thursday, Naomi took me to my first counselling at the local hospital's mental health hub. I wondered if it was the same place the paramedics had taken Mabel.

The waiting room had whitewashed walls with various garish paintings of suns and rainbows, supposedly to create a happy atmosphere.

Naomi guided me through to the right room when we were called. A woman sat behind a table. She had kind, twinkling eyes and a short brown bob. I read from her badge that her name was Dr Mainwaring.

"Hello! You must be Ellen. Please take a seat," she said in an overly cheery manner.

I did as she said; Naomi taking one adjacent to me. The seat was soft and dented from years of use; the outside like old sacking.

Dr Mainwaring shifted through a pile of typed notes. I knew they were about me. I felt exposed that this stranger knew every detail of my scars. She talked to me for a while, starting off with small talk, before advancing to deep, personal questions. I felt the blood run to my face as she read my wounds, taking notes. My answers became short and reluctant, watching the ballpoint pen scribe across the notepad.

At the end of the session, Dr Mainwaring asked me to go back to the waiting room whilst she 'had a chat' with Naomi.

I listened, my ear pressed against the door, hating them discussing me. I heard Naomi saying 'hallucinations' and 'trauma-inflicted', and Dr Mainwaring responding with 'PTSD' and 'sleeping issues'.

"It's not unusual for people with such traumatic pasts to have experiences like these. Ellen will improve, but with the unimaginable thing she has gone through, she will be impacted with PTSD for weeks, months, years. Time can help, along with therapy, but the road ahead for her mental health is uncertain."

When I heard the shuffle of chairs, I bolted back to the waiting room. Naomi smiled when she saw me, but her eyes were bloodshot and sad.

I continued to have meetings with the Brown family. One day we had a picnic at the park, and the next we went to play crazy golf. Sometimes, I even stayed over at their house with Naomi, until, one day, I was told it was time for me to try and move in.

I gave Naomi a big hug and managed to thank her properly for the first time. She squeezed me back; her eyes watering.

"This isn't goodbye though, Ellen. You can always pop in and see me whenever you like."

She waved me off as Helen drove me in the car to start a new chapter of my life.

Life since moving in with the Brown family has been very different. In a good way.

Mostly.

I can't explain the feeling of safety and warmth, living with a proper family. I struggled to take umbrage with them for my own mum. I still loved her, but didn't miss the life I had before.

I now had my own bedroom. I beamed with joy when I saw it, as I'd never even had a bed most of my childhood. It was just a little box room, but Amy and Tim had turned it into a little palace. All four walls were painted a creamy rose, with a wall sticker of a big blossom tree. The room smelled heavenly too, as Amy had bought special scented sticks in a little glass jug.

I had a mega wardrobe, and when I opened it, I found several new outfits. And, best of all, my bed had a crocheted quilt that Amy had helped Zoe to make.

Since the day in Pizza Express, I daren't even breathe a word about Zoe and her silent suffering. She always seemed to be in an eerie mood, drifting around the house, her face blank and her eyes melancholic as she stared endlessly into the screen of her phone.

I knew she was constantly being hurt and I wanted to help, but I was scared of hurting her even more.

How could you hold a girl together if she was already shattered into a thousand shards?

Tim let me have a go on his cello. It seemed such an alarmingly big instrument that it was a bit overwhelming.

Tim laughed.

"Wait until you see a double bass!"

I wasn't quite sure what that was, but I was glad I'd amused him.

However, nobody laughed when I played it, carefully moving the bow across the strings. I was hesitant, the first time. The strings vibrated slightly against my hand. I shivered as it let out a low timbre; sad and yearning. I experimented again on the lower strings, whilst adding a tune, using my index finger to slide out on the strings.

Amy looked shocked, Tim was baffled, and Zoe clapped!

"You're amazing, Ellen!" she said, catching my eye with hers for a brief second, casting stars into my soul.

"She certainly is!" said Amy.

"We'll have to get you proper lessons, Ellen," said Tim.

His voice was thick, and his eyes misty, almost as though he was choked up.

After that, Tim would sit with me and I would practise every morning, sometimes later on as well. It felt so natural and freeing to lose myself in the cello. The cello felt like a part of me...a part so new and unhurt, with no history, just a future. It gave me the feeling and sound of hope.

A few days later I found Zoe lying on her bed, with her head buried in her pillow when Amy and Tim were out at the shops. The duvet felt quite sodden and warm. She must have been crying a lot before I went in. Her phone was flung by her side, the screen glowing open on a chat. I laid my hand on her arm. She didn't object.

"Hey, it's OK!" I tried to convince her.

She looked up at me. Her eyes were startlingly crimson and bloodshot, her face was like an exploded red-ink pen, and her nose was running. This was a shock, as I had rarely seen Zoe this upset before. I looked down at her phone screen, then before I could stop myself, I took it from the bed and scrolled through the messages. The chat read 'Ava' at the top, with an emoji of two best friends. There were really awful things written, not just from Ava. It was clear Zoe had got wound up and had lashed out in words.

"This is awful," I said.

Zoe gave a moan and feebly attempted to snatch her phone back, but she was too weak and I held on.

There was a video.

It had been sent today. I saw it had been clumsily recorded, but one person was definite – Zoe. She was in the middle of the frame, her eyes wild with fire, her face deep with sadness, before she punched out, tears streaming down her face.

"Who's this, Zoe?" I trembled.

She didn't need to tell me.

"Emily," she breathed.

"Oh, Ellen, please don't tell mum!" she begged, clinging on to my arm.

"Well, I really think I should, Zoe. But if you really don't want me to, I won't."

"Oh, Ellen! She said such horrid things," Zoe spluttered, a fresh waterfall cascading down her cheeks.

"She threw white spirit over me and said I should kill myself!" she whimpered, before hiding back under her pillow.

"Zoe, that really isn't acceptable! She can't hurt you in this way! We need to tell Amy."

"NO!" Zoe cut me off.

"If I tell anyone she'll show that video to the police. Assault is illegal, Ellen. Free speech isn't."

"Zoe, I have your back. I promise I will do what I can for you. Please think about telling your mum and dad."

I went into the kitchen and whispered to Tim, who, by this time, had returned from the shops with Amy.

He looked solemn and nodded. He helped me carry the bulky case into Zoe's room to set up.

Then, when he had gone, I started - a low, melancholic note fading into a sad tune, with a needle of hope. I gradually made the simple tune merge into a happy one, using higher notes and quicker bowing.

Zoe was smiling now, inquisitive, most of her tears dry by the time I finished the last note. She didn't need to say anything, but in the way she looked into my eyes, I knew she might like me a little bit. And maybe trust me a bit.

Chapter 13

Zoe

Things are so different since Ellen moved in.

It's not just her being there; it's all the change. Wherever I go, she is there - at the kitchen table eating cereal or sitting demurely on the sofa watching 'Peppa Pig'. It's crazy because she is an adult in so many ways, yet she will often revert to infancy. I suppose it's because she was robbed of some of her childhood, so she desperately tries to relive it. I told Ellen that Peppa Pig was a programme for three-year-olds, but I think it was the simple, loving family routines which attracted her. How Mummy Pig and Daddy Pig tucked up their children in bed each night and read them a story. I knew little of Ellen's previous life, but from the grave conversations of mum and dad it seemed unlikely she had had any bed to sleep on, let alone a bedtime story.

Talking of sleep, I can't get that any more! Ellen is on dad's cello every morning, without fail, for at least half an hour, obsessively playing exercises and tunes over and over again. Dad always tried to get me to play it, but to be truthful, I found it boring, just making the simplest scratchy noises, and couldn't be bothered to read the squiggles on the page. I wanted to play *real* music now.

It was annoying to see Ellen's patience and natural flair. To be truthful, I was jealous. *I* wanted to do something special. *I* wanted to be praised. *I* was mum and dad's actual daughter, so why wasn't I the favourite?

Things hadn't calmed down with Emily either. It was terrifying how she could stalk me wherever I went. I couldn't even get a break outside of school because she would be there, on my Instagram or Snapchat. I tried numerous times to block or delete her, but she always found ways round it, making new accounts or fake numbers. I was scared of being left out of anything, and always hoped things would improve.

The weeks ran by, and it seemed like Ellen had been living with us forever. I thought I would hate Ellen, but, even though I didn't want to admit it, I was actually beginning to like her.

Ava's birthday was on Sunday. Though she had assured me she was having no celebrations, I still wanted to give her something special because she was my best friend in the world - or at least that's what I thought. We couldn't afford anything *really* special and expensive, with the extra cost of life and Ellen, as payment to foster carers barely covers anything. I shouted at her for that, as in my eyes, it was her fault I couldn't get my best friend the birthday present she wanted. Yet again, I had made Ellen cry, and mum and dad sent me to my room. Once I'd calmed down, I felt truly awful. I'm not very good at saying sorry, but I tried my best and even managed to give Ellen a hug and recorded a dance video with her, both of us waving our arms and laughing hysterically. She looked at me with such gratitude that I wanted to cry.

I spent ages on Ava's presents, eventually choosing a pot of shiny glass beads, and embroidery floss that I carefully threaded and knotted to make a bracelet. I spent an equal amount of time on her card, drawing the two of us, our arms round each other, with what I thought was a sophisticated message inside. I couldn't find anything to wrap the presents in, and it was too late to buy anything, but I decided it didn't matter too much and placed the card and gifts inside a faded Christmas bottle bag I found when rummaging around at the back of the cupboard. I blush now with sheer anger, and cringe. I had made that clumsy bracelet and card with such love and hope. It had made my hands flap with excitement to imagine Ava's face when she saw them - the happiness I could give to my friend.

"Hey, mum, can I go round to Ava's to drop off her birthday presents?" I asked.

"Hmm..." mum said, emerging from the kitchen in her big flowery apron, with worms of dough sticking to the hair on her arms.

"OK, but don't be too long as I want to take Sally for a walk around the park."

"Amy! Amy, look! I've made a cookie dog with chocolate-chip eyes! Oh, it looks just like Sally! Wait until Zoe sees it!" wafted a shrill excited voice.

I vaguely heard mum congratulating her as I walked out of the door. The wind hit my face like ice, frosting my cheeks and making my eyes stream. I'd forgotten to put gloves on, so the December weather attacked my hands, chilling them to the bone. Ava's was only a 10-minute walk from my house, yet it seemed like a whole world away. She lived in a proper house with its own garden. My whole childhood had been spent living in a block of flats with an equally bleak communal square of shabby grass.

I had to pass the shops before I got to the estate. Smells of Burger King and KFC, along with a Yak & Yeti curry house, mingled with each other in the air, each smell becoming more individual and disgusting as I passed them. The last fast food place in town was the classic McDonald's; the fluorescent yellow 'M' sitting on top of the roof, tinted grey and dismal - the perfect mood for the scene. It would have been even better if it had been raining or thundering, but the sky was a sheet of plain and calm white.

And there they were.

Through the window I saw paper burger boxes and soggy chips littering the table, along with cups of milkshake, with straws shrivelled at the top with saliva. There was a girl sat at the head of the table. It couldn't be...NO! I leaned in, closer to the glass, with my forehead pressed against it, for once not caring about the germs. There were Ava, Emily and James - my whole 'friendship' group - sitting around, obviously enjoying Ava's birthday...without me!

Despite it being early December, Emily was showing enough flesh to be on a beach. Her sparkling blue eyes caught mine, and they shone with glee, and she mouthed that one terrible word at me.

"Loser!"

I suddenly felt rage rising inside me; my stomach a tight fist of anger, and my sadness molten and unpredictable. My head was spinning with months of pent-up emotion. I was fed up of letting them walk all over me. I am screaming every day and nobody hears a thing! I was going to make them hear. I would cause a stir!

I ran straight through the door to their table and stood there, panting, as they all stared at me, dumbfounded.

"Zoe...I can explain," started Ava, her voice ridden with nervous guilt.

"No, you don't need to," I spat, contemptuously.

Emily raised her eyebrows at me; her Cupid's bow mouth forming a smirk.

There were a few seconds of silence, when all I could hear was my pulse beating my eardrums, like a time bomb about to explode.

"Why didn't you invite me?" I whispered directly at Ava.

Another silence.

Tick. Tick. Tick.

She looked a little bit sorry for me and opened her mouth again, but the words got stuck in her throat. I saw Emily nudge Ava and whisper in her ear, then they all looked at me, eyebrows raised, in silent laughter.

Ava looked around at all her friends, strong and happy, and then at me, neglected and alone. She took a deep breath. It was an obvious choice for her to make...the easy option.

"I didn't invite you because you're a FREAK, Zoe! Face it, everybody hates you, and you've been a bitch to poor Emily."

I shook in stunned silence.

Tick. Tick. Tick.

Everyone smiled at Ava, and I knew in that moment I had been betrayed. I gave them all one last look and blundered like fire out of the door to the alley behind McDonald's. I heard footsteps behind me and quickly turned on my heels.

"Emily," I spat, my lungs knotted, anger controlling me like roaring flames.

"Are you OK, Zoe?" she asked, in a falsely nice tone.

"What do you think?!" I hissed, my eyes burning, barbed wire stabbing my throat.

Then she ducked nearer, whispering venom into my ears.

"You know, I really don't blame Ava. If you were my friend, I wouldn't be inviting a loser bitch like you to my party just to spoil everything. Ava told me about all the sleepovers you insisted on having, where you had a tantrum and went home at 2 in the morning!"

She laughed with glee.

"You know Ava's having a massive rave-up party tonight in the village hall? The whole class is coming - even the boys - oh, I forgot, apart from freaks and bitches. The world would be a better place without you, Zoe Brown, because you're a loser!"

I knew she was talking nonsense. She was the vacuous bitch I had always despised. The girl whose head was no deeper than a puddle. The snake who hides behind a mask of popularity whilst breaking you apart.

Shit!

Of course she was talking nonsense...and yet, what if it was true? Ava had sworn blind against the texts against me to Emily, so I had assumed she had used an app to fake them...but then, why hadn't she invited me? Why? Why? WHY?

And then the molten anger exploded.

My hand shot out with full force and I punched Emily smack on the mouth. To my amazement she fell down immediately; helpless. Now was my chance; my only shot of revenge.

I had the power.

I jumped on her, scratching at her perfect face, tearing at her perfect hair, punching and kicking at her perfect body. I felt her weaken. I felt the anger subside. Then I screamed as I saw what I had done. The scratches on her face, the punches on her arms, the bloodied nose and mouth. The world whirled around me as I turned to run...and I saw Ava standing by the wall, recording it all on her phone.

I blundered straight through the crowds of people, through the town, through the estate, until I was in the park. All the time my face was on fire, a glowing halo of guilt framing me. I struggled through the bushes to my secret place. The trees were almost bare now, with piles of orange and crimson scattered on the ground whilst shrivelled brown leaves lay silently underneath, decaying into mud, and in that moment I felt like them. All the good times were over and now I was mud, and nobody wanted me near them.

A loser. A nobody. A FREAK.

I screamed with rage and hurled the bottle bag containing Ava's presents on to the ground and stamped on it until it was flat, amazed I had bothered to grab it after everything that had happened. Then I took out the card and ripped it to shreds until all that was left was the bitter memory.

Chapter 14

Ellen

"Zoe, are you OK?" I asked her, as she caked her face in make-up.

"Won't you get told off for that at school?"

"It's the last day, Ellen. We're allowed to wear what we like," she snapped at me. I could tell she was stressed. Really stressed.

She peered agonisingly into her bedroom mirror, then at her phone, at the make-up tutorial on YouTube. Zoe never wore make-up, so why was she suddenly bothering now?

"Look, Ellen. Do I look OK?" she asked, turning to me.

"Err...honestly?"

I didn't know what to say. She had raided Amy's dressing table, so the foundation colour didn't match her skin, and she had applied it much too thickly anyway, so it was starting to crack. Her eyes were outlined with a black felt-tip, as she couldn't find an eyeliner, and her lashes were stiff with mascara.

"Um," I said, not wanting to say the wrong thing.

If I told her it was good, she would go to school and be humiliated. If I didn't, I might shatter her confidence even more.

"It's...not really you," I said, trying to be tactful.

"Good!" she said. "I need to show them."

"Show them what, Zoe?"

"Show them I've changed. I'm not a freak. Make them like me," she said, opening her wardrobe and discarding most of its contents on the floor.

"Ugh," she groaned. "Why are all my outfits so babyish?"

I inwardly burned at this. Zoe had a whole wardrobe of clothes; I had barely any not so long ago.

"Sorry," she said, realising what had left her mouth.

"It's OK. Look, why don't you wear that denim skirt with your Christmas jumper?" I offered.

"That denim skirt comes down to my knees, and I'd never hear the end of it if I wore a Christmas jumper, Ellen," she sighed, deeply and sadly.

"Why don't we go and eat breakfast and then you decide what to wear?"

After a lot of persuading, she agreed.

Amy was already up in her dressing gown, sipping a big mug of tea.

"Good morning, girls," said Amy half-heartedly, typing on her laptop. She then took a proper look at Zoe.

"Zoe! What on earth?! Is that my bronze foundation? And you've used my best lipstick!"

"Only because you wouldn't buy me any make-up."

"Zoe, you know that's not true. I'm happy to buy you make-up, but you've always been adamant you don't want it!"

"Yeah, well I've changed my mind."

"Zoe, I'm not trying to be mean, but if you walk into school like that, you'll likely frighten everyone!"

"So...you can't stop me!" Zoe said, though I could tell she was uncertain now.

"Look, Zoe, I'm too tired for an argument. Go and wash it off and then get dressed."

Zoe opened her mouth to argue but then subsided, knowing she was beaten, and sloped off to the bathroom. When she returned, her face was bright red from scrubbing. Not just her face, either. Her eyes were bloodshot, like she had been crying.

Then I saw what she was wearing and blinked. She was just wearing a vest on top, and she had tied it up, so it showed all of her tummy. The skirt was another matter. I don't know where she dug it out from, but it looked years old and equally too small, barely covering her.

Amy sighed.

"Zoe, what on earth are you wearing?" she asked, irritated.

"Clothes!" Zoe replied, trying to act cool.

"For goodness' sake, Zoe, it's December, not summer! And even if it was, I wouldn't let you go out in that. I can see your underwear!"

Zoe blushed and tried to pull down the tiny skirt.

"It's what everybody else wears, mum," she said, a little thickly. But she went and got changed all the same, returning in a pair of jeans and a black V-neck jumper.

"Why don't you wear your Christmas jumper?" asked Amy, a little hurt.

"Mum!" moaned Zoe, rolling her eyes.

"Snap out of that attitude, Zoe, I'm warning you," said Amy, sniffing the air. "Oh gawd, the toast!" she moaned, unplugging the toaster and fishing out the charcoaled slice with a knife. She then peered at the kitchen clock.

"You'll have to have cereal, Zoe," she said, bringing out the packet from the cupboard.

We ate in unison.

Well, I ate.

Zoe just had a couple of mouthfuls and stirred the cornflakes into mush.

"Amy, can we walk Zoe to school?" I asked, crunching up the last of my cornflakes, desperate to make sure Zoe was OK.

"Actually, that's not a bad idea, Ellen. I need to walk Sally and pop into Smiths. We could do that on the way back, if that's OK with you, Zoe? It will be good for you to get used to the school route as well, Ellen, seeing as you'll be doing it soon."

"Really? That is so embarrassing," Zoe pretended to moan, but I could tell she was actually pleased.

"Remember, we are putting up the Christmas decorations later!" said Amy.

"Oh, yes!" I replied, my eyes sparkling. I was so excited about Christmas, mainly because I'd never had a proper one before. Santa certainly hadn't visited our flat much.

"Zoe! We're leaving in five minutes!" Amy called, loudly.

"Come and get your coat and shoes on, Ellen."

As I walked over, my foot stepped into something warm and squelchy. I looked down.

"Yuck!" I said, jerking back my foot and hopping up and down.

"Ellen, what is it, darling?" Amy called, before coming to me.

"Oh dear, not again! I've already cleared up one lot of dog sick this morning."

"What?" snapped Zoe, returning to the room.

"Oh, mum, is Sally OK? We need to take her to the vets!" she panicked.

"Look, Zoe, I'm sure she's fine. She probably just ate some grass or something. If she's sick again, I promise I'll phone the vets, OK?" Amy said hastily, although I could tell she didn't really mean it.

But Zoe was barely listening. She was kneeling down at Sally's dog basket, fondling her grey ears and crooning to her.

"Right, Ellen, go and rinse your foot with the shower head and put on a clean pair of socks, and Zoe, Sally's absolutely fine. Stop worrying! She's just...getting a bit older."

By the time I'd washed and changed, Amy and Zoe were all ready to go.

"Come on, Sally!" Amy sang out. "Walkies!"

Sally looked at her from across the room, her brown eyes deep and wise. Then, very slowly, she rose from her basket and padded across the room on her snowy paws, each step clearly an effort.

When we were finally out of the house, we were already running late, due to the shenanigans of that morning.

Amy held my hand and the three of us sped along the pavements, with Sally limping behind. I noticed how Zoe didn't say anything all the way, and her face had gone ghostly pale.

"Are you alright, Zoe?"

"Fine!" she snapped at me. I knew there was definitely something wrong.

I saw the school building loom into view, tall and ominous against the morning sky. Zoe let go of Amy's hand and marched forwards, trying to look confident and composed. Even if I was the only person who could see it, I knew she wasn't.

"Bye, Zoe!" Amy called, as Zoe walked off into the fire of the school grounds, her shoulders hunched and her neck bent. Invisible.

"Amy..." I hesitated. "Can we just watch...to make sure Zoe's OK?" I asked, peering into the playing courts.

"That is such a lovely idea, Ellen, poppet, but I don't think Zoe would appreciate it if she saw us nosing into her school life. I'm sure she'll be fine," said Amy, tugging on my hand, but I wasn't listening.

As she spoke, I saw.

I saw it all.

The moment she stepped into the school playground all the noise stopped, as though the whole world had been put on pause.

I saw Zoe, in the middle of it all, like she was the only thing that existed - a rainbow in the sky, and yet all they saw was a thundercloud.

And then it started.

They surrounded her, shouting and gossiping. Getting out their phones and playing the video, again and again. I saw another girl. She was tall and shapely, with long blonde hair and a sickening expression. She had a sling on her arm and plasters on her face. I didn't need to be told who she was.

The crowd parted as she entered the scene, with dozens of arms hugging her.

I saw Zoe, as she crumpled on the floor, sobbing and defeated.

"Ellen...?"

It was Amy, gently tugging at my arm.

"She's fine, darl..." but her voice drifted away as she saw too.

"Zoe!" she stuttered, and jerked her body as if to run to her, before stopping.

Just at that moment a scary-looking man stepped out of the building, his dominance made clear as the pupils scattered. He was tall and menacing, in a casual suit, and I watched as he advanced towards Zoe, bending down next to her.

"You!" he boomed at her, although she was right next to him.

Zoe didn't flinch.

"Inside, now! The police are waiting!"

This time Zoe jerked, and tried to run, but as she looked round she realised there was nowhere to go.

"NO!" she screamed at him, sobbing, as he marched her towards the door.

Then her foot shot out and she kicked him hard on the shin. He suddenly stopped in shock with the strength of the kick and Zoe ran full speed towards the gate, tears streaming down her face.

She ran straight past us, her eyes wild and determined like two balls of fire. Sally howled and strained at her lead, whimpering, as Zoe became a blur in the distance.

Chapter 15

Zoe

I had my back turned to them all, my lips sealed, arms hugging my knees, whilst the lady kept asking me question after question, drilling into my brain.

I didn't like the questions. They delved deep into the most vulnerable parts - parts that I had never talked about before.

Police came, and they all wanted to talk to me to find out the answers - the truth.

Lips zipped, don't say a word.

I hated the fact they would write down anything I said, as though I was in a court case, like Ellen.

In the end, they let me off with a caution.

Mum and dad were there, too. Mum was crying quietly and dad was very red in the face. Ellen had gone to Naomi's.

Mum sniffed; dad coughed.

Then there was silence.

"What happened on Sunday? It's important you tell us. Apparently, you attacked another girl in your year behind a building," the lady said, reading from her notes.

"Do you feel angry?" asked the lady, softly.

Angry? Angry?!

'Angry' definitely wasn't the right word for the torrent of tangled emotions rioting inside my head.

Why had I even gone to school the next day? If I hadn't, maybe they wouldn't have found out.

Shattered. Defeated. Unmendable.

Lips shut, eyes closed, don't talk.

"Do you want to write it down, Zoe?"

No. Lips shut, eyes sealed.

The school had suspended me, so mum and dad kept dragging me to these sessions day after day until I was 'stable'.

I didn't talk. I barely ate.

Eventually, after a fortnight or so, the psychiatrist asked mum and dad to stay in the room whilst I waited outside. I listened, of course.

"Mr and Mrs Brown," she addressed them, formally.

I heard mum take a deep breath.

"Obviously, this isn't an official diagnosis, and we can arrange further tests."

Diagnosis? Tests?

I wasn't ill.

I WASN'T crazy! *I WASN'T!*

"Mr and Mrs Brown, I think without doubt your daughter is on the ASD spectrum, and I would recommend further counselling and anger management to start with."

There was crying from mum...and, possibly, dad.

No. No.

Autism spectrum disorder.

I didn't have a DISORDER!

I wasn't autistic.

Autism was a mental illness that crazy people had. But then...was I crazy?

Images of the past few months flashed through my head. Under the kayak at Ashwood Forest. Punching Emily over and over again in the recent pain of being betrayed. The uncontrollable power I had to hurt people. The constant knot of anxiety. The drilling of thoughts bombarding my ears. Fireworks exploding inside me. Always the effort to be the same.

I remembered being hunched up under the duvet on my phone, Googling websites, not being able to bear the answers I found. Because it was the truth. And the truth is painful.

Was I autistic?

Mum and dad came out of the room, wan and tear-stained, although when they saw me, they painted false smiles on their lips.

I didn't want to talk to anyone.

There were too many emotions; too many thoughts. I wanted to get them out, but...

No! I mustn't lash out. I'm NOT crazy!

In that moment I wanted just one thing: to be normal. I wanted to talk to nobody. Just to curl up with Sally and whisper all my worries into her grey ear whilst she thumped her tail. Ever since I was three-years-old, Sally had been loyal and faithful to me. Always there to talk to, always there to listen. Always, without fail, making me feel better.

I burst into the flat and called for her in a croaky voice.

I sobbed into her peppered fur, feeling numb with emotion. She thumped her tail and licked my salty cheeks, making me chuckle, then I grabbed her lead and ran with her to the park. Alone.

Chapter 16

Ellen

Zoe wouldn't talk to anyone.

Everybody thought it would be best for me to go back to Naomi's for a while, but I was adamant I was staying. I had been searching my whole life to find a home with a caring family. Now I had succeeded, I didn't want to give it all up, though I did end up having to stay with Naomi for a week or so when Zoe was at her worst.

Christmas came as a break, with joy for us all. I loved the sparkle - it was everywhere! On Christmas Eve, Tim drove us to some hills which seemed like the countryside, and we took Sally for a long walk. I loved how cosy and lovable everything was; there was so much joy that we could almost forget.

I heard about Zoe's diagnosis. I didn't understand why everybody was making such an embarrassed fuss about it. Zoe was still the same person, wearing the same skin she always had.

Back at the flat, Zoe and I made mince pies, whilst Tim and Amy boiled mulled wine. I saw Zoe grin whilst she rolled and shaped, and her eyes twinkled as we flicked flour at each other - the room was filled with sparkle and spice. I had thought hard about Christmas presents, in the end choosing two packs of clay and acrylic paint. I fashioned a jewellery tray for Amy, and a coffee coaster for Tim. I spent ages on Zoe's gift, fashioning a clay labrador to go on her bedside table, carefully painting its coat to get the salt-and-pepper effect of Sally's fur.

That evening, we all sat in the living room, wrapping presents and chatting merrily. I suddenly wondered what mum's Christmas would be like. Living and breathing in the cell of the secure unit she was at.

No. Don't think about mum, it just spoils everything.

Zoe insisted on wrapping up bones for Sally, which she hid amongst other gifts under the tree. Sally immediately went and started sniffing under the tree, thumping her tail with glee. Amy sighed, happily: "I told you she would sniff them out, Zoe! Go and hide them somewhere she can't reach."

I suddenly wondered if Amy and Tim had got Zoe a gift. Since all the incidents, there had been a sad and stressful mist in the air, and they talked to Zoe in a new, disappointed tone. Zoe was still having therapy sessions every week, which she utterly detested, and refused to cooperate in.

On Christmas morning, I woke very early and couldn't get back to sleep. I kept tossing and turning, wondering about the future. I crept into Zoe's room, surprised to find her awake, scrolling through her phone.

"Merry Christmas, Zoe," I whispered.

"Merry Christmas, Ellen," she whispered back, quickly switching off her phone.

"I couldn't sleep," I said, unnecessarily.

"Me neither," said Zoe, yawning. "But then that's nothing new."

She switched on her bedside lamp. One of her gerbils looked startled and scurried underground at the sudden brightness. Zoe chuckled.

"That's how I feel," she said in a light-hearted tone, but as her words tailed off I could feel a darkness to them.

"Come on, let's watch some Netflix, Zoe."

Recently, Zoe and I had been finding great fun in watching teen series and arguing over the outcomes. We would often sit still, talking on the sofa long after the credits rolled.

"OK, but don't you dare tell me he should break up with Kyla!"

We both giggled. It felt so good. So good to laugh and talk about nothing. To have the freedom to be able to concentrate on such little things like the hottest boy in a Netflix series, instead of when or if the next meal would be, or how I would ration the allowance.

We hadn't even got halfway through the episode without bickering gleefully, which ended in a pillow fight.

Amy came into the room, gently scolding us.

"Girls, it's scarcely six in the morning and the house is already in turmoil!"

"Merry Christmas, mum!" Zoe said quickly.

She caught my eye and we exploded into laughter.

"Well, seeing as you're up, you might as well see what Santa has brought you!"

"Oh, mum...seriously?" said Zoe, pretending to be embarrassed.

I obviously knew Santa wasn't real, but there was still something magical about everything, stuffing sweets into our mouths and lazily singing Christmas songs. Everything felt so...warm.

I couldn't help worrying about mum, though I tried my hardest to forget, just for one day. I felt so guilty at all the wonderful warmth, as Mabel lay cold and stiff in some hard, regulation freezer.

Tim, Zoe and I went to the park to walk Sally, whilst Amy prepared Christmas dinner. The wind was bitterly cold, so I pulled my coat tightly around me. Zoe ran ahead, discarding her jumper and running short-sleeved through the grass. I thought Tim would scold her, but he just shook his head.

"That girl will be the death of me," he laughed, but I could feel the sadness in his voice.

Zoe circled back, with Sally several paces behind, and pulled on her thick sweater. Her cheeks were bright red.

"Aren't you cold, Zoe?" I asked.

"Yeah," she shrugged. "That's the point - it just makes me feel...real, I suppose."

When we returned to the flat, Amy was starting to dish up Christmas dinner. Zoe gave an irritated look at the steaming turkey that Amy was carving, its juices dripping.

"There's a nut roast for you in the oven, Zoe," Amy sighed. "Christmas is once a year, so stop judging the rest of us, please."

"But, mum, how would you like it if your only purpose in life was to be killed? Reared with false hope of life, before one day somebody slaughters you..." Zoe trailed off, her eyes deep.

"Quit it, Zoe, or you can go to your room. I am not having you spoil Ellen's first Christmas with us!" Amy said, as she carried on carving the turkey.

I remembered the Christmases I'd had in the past. Mum had always said it was a stupid excuse to spend money we didn't have, however, she would always use the season as a reason to drink.

Amy had bought a Christmas pudding, which Zoe insisted on lighting with Tim's brandy – something he was not too pleased about. As I watched the eerie blue flames dance among the currants, I wished. I wished that everyday could be as happy as today.

Zoe had only toyed with her food, taking tiny portions and complaining about the fat on the potatoes, or the richness of the cream, looking down anxiously at her stomach.

After we had all finished, we went and sat in the living room to open our gifts. I saw Zoe give the biggest smile I had seen all day, and she hugged me tight as she unwrapped the clay Sally. Amy and Tim were equally touched by their gifts, which surprised me, as the coaster was wonky and the jewellery tray lumpy, but I realise now it was the heartfelt thought that counted. It was slightly awkward as Zoe had many parcels from relatives and aunties, but Amy and Tim had filled in with extra trinkets for me; a necklace with an 'E' pendant; various bath bombs and soaps; and a mug with musical notes swirling on the paintwork. Zoe gave me a pair of fluffy socks and peppermint hot chocolate powder. I was surprised at the last package, when I opened the paper and found a phone lying inside. I fingered it, nervously.

"We thought it may be useful, so you can keep in touch with your friends and be a part of things. We had to speak to Helen, and there are safeguarding locks on certain things, but we feel you are very trustworthy," said Amy, smiling.

I thanked her feverishly, but I was already distracted with her sentence. *Keep in touch with your friends and be a part of things.* I only knew Zoe. I had no other friends, so I couldn't be a part of anything. I felt sick as I realised the hunch she was getting at, and couldn't shake it off or ask if it were true.

On Boxing Day, I got up early and pulled on my best skirt and top, wanting to look good. I brushed my hair and gingerly added mascara to my lashes, desperate to make her proud. At the same time, I also wanted to just get back into bed. I stroked the wrapping paper of the gift I had so carefully sculpted; a mother and daughter, hugging. I had carefully painted the girl's hair mousy brown and tried to make the woman beautiful. I so hoped mum would like it. Helen tried to make conversation all the way, but it gradually petered out into silence as we approached the bleak, grey building.

Psychiatric secure unit.

Helen turned to me.

"It's natural to be nervous, Ellen, but remember I will be there and we can leave at any point. Don't be alarmed if your mum is not quite...how you remember."

I just nodded, scared one word would open the stitches so delicately binding me.

"Can I help you? Are you looking for anywhere in particular?" a man asked.

Helen glanced at the sheet of paper she was holding.

"We're looking for Miss Maclaren," she said, showing him the paper.

"Ah yes, she is actually in a separate room in a more secure area to our other residents, given the circumstances. I'll take you to see her," he said, beckoning us to follow him.

After several flights of stairs and more doors that he needed to use his special card to open, we got to my mum's room.

"Mum!" I said desperately as he opened the door, eager to see her.

I stopped as I got to the bed, wondering if he had got the wrong room. The bedraggled woman on the bed had sour skin and smelled of piss; her hair brittle and sallow. She seemed to have aged a decade, and her face was lifeless.

"Mum!" I said again, shaking her shoulder.

"She may be a bit woozy just now as she had another dose of her meds this morning," said the man.

I saw the woman's lids open, exposing a pair of bloodshot eyes. At first, she gave a glazed expression, until her eyes caught mine. I saw her darken; those two eyes just staring into my soul. I realised she knew. She knew everything and I was overcome by a wave of betrayal. I desperately tried to explain myself, petering off until I promised we would be back together soon. Mum didn't react. She just carried on staring at me.

"Why don't you show her the lovely present you made, Ellen," said Helen, handing it to me.

I nervously handed the parcel to mum, smiling. She made no attempt to open the wrapping, so I opened it for her, exposing the clay sculpture. It was at this point I realised how awful it was, as if looking at it through a new set of eyes - the uneven shapes and messy paintwork.

"Look, mum, it's me and you, an' we're hugging," I said, handing it to her. "I love you, mum."

Mum's hand reached out. It was the first time she had moved since I arrived. She grasped the sculpture in her fist before hurling it at the floor. I watched as the clay broke and crumbled, and I just sat by the fragments, sobbing.

Chapter 17

Ellen

Since October, Amy had been homeschooling me, with advice from the authorities, as she had done some part-time teaching a few years before. In February, it was planned that I would go part-time to school with Zoe. I wasn't sure how I felt about that. I remember the times when I did go to school. People would pull faces and hold their noses, saying I smelled, or that I had greasy hair. They were probably right. Even before drugs, mum was such a scatty, wild sort of mum you couldn't rely on her to get things done.

Reading was another matter. The words jumped and danced on the page, and I couldn't make sense of them. It was no better now. I heard Amy and Tim whispering about me getting a diagnosis for dyslexia. I hated the way I was turning into a pin board, with labels being stuck to me. I don't think Zoe was that happy, either. I heard her whispering to Amy in the kitchen when she thought I was in my room.

"Please, mum. This is my fresh start. I am really going to go in there and be a different person. People think I'm 'retarded' enough, without Ellen!"

I shook with sheer hurt that she could talk about me in this way.

"Zoe! How dare you speak about Ellen in that way! I'm disgusted with you. That poor girl has been through shit you and I could never bear, and your first thought is how it will affect YOU?"

"No, mum! Of course that's not what I meant!" Zoe said as she started to cry.

"Then what did you mean, you selfish girl?!"

"I just...thought it might be better for her to go to a different school and make her own path."

"What different school? Cradisfield is the only half-decent one around these parts, and you'll need to look after her. She's going with you two mornings and one day a week to start with, and there's special support being put in place for her. That's final."

I hated the word 'special'. It sounded so patronising.

The week after February half-term, Amy took me to have a meeting with the headmaster, Mr Anderson. I remember Zoe describing him like a mole with little beady eyes, always lurking in his hovel of an office. To be honest, I think it is a very accurate description.

"Ah, hello, Mrs Brown," he said as we entered, lining up papers on his desk.

He squinted at Amy in a knowing way, as if they had met before – it was probably to do with the incidents before Christmas.

"And you must be Ellen?" Mr Anderson said, shaking my hand.

I felt embarrassed as my palm was icy and wet from nerves, and I saw him discreetly wipe his own hand on his trouser leg after the encounter.

"So, Ellen, I hear that you will be part-time, enrolling for a few mornings a week and perhaps one full day, given your sensitive circumstances."

He looked at me. It felt as if his little eyes could see into the darkest depths of my past; the intent stubble of his beard making me cringe.

"I hear you haven't had much previous schooling?"

I shook my head. I remembered my long-ago school days, which came few and far between as mum was trying to subtly pull me out. When school rang and asked where I was after about a month of absence, which mum had been ill through, she said we had moved away and concocted some sort of story that they swallowed.

"Well, please do not worry. We have plenty of support that can be put in place to help you catch up."

"Ta," I said, blankly, nerves making me revolve back to my old street language.

"You're currently being fostered by Mr and Mrs Brown, parents of Zoe Brown, am I right?"

I nodded.

"Would you like to be in the same tutor group as Zoe, so she can look after you? Or we could arrange somebody else?"

"I want to be with Zoe," I said, cutting in quickly and firmly.

Mr Anderson nodded, his gnarled fingers scribbling down notes.

"That means your tutor group will be 9M3, and your tutor will be Mr Macclesfield. After you have done the little quiz I'm about to give you, we can arrange for you to meet him and I'll give you a tour around."

"Quiz?" I said, my heart beating fast.

"Yes, just so we can gauge which classes will be best suited to you," he said, now rummaging around in a chest of drawers, out of which he pulled a stapled little booklet and pen, before placing them on his desk.

"Now, before we get on to that, we need to have a conversation about the support that can be put in place for you."

He read through his notes.

"I understand with your court hearing coming up in the next few months, things may be particularly stressful for you, Ellen, and it's very important we make this big step as manageable as possible for you."

I felt sick to my stomach, clamping my hands. Everything was so fast, so new, and felt like I was backing into a den of fire.

"We have a small site in the school dedicated to the wellbeing of our students. It's to the side of the art block. There are lots of trained teachers in there, as well as professional councillors and calming environments. We call it our 'wellbeing block' and you are welcome to go here anytime you feel like things are...maybe not going so well. I'll show you after your little quiz."

I had heard Zoe talk about the wellbeing block. The school had tried to get her to go in there after her diagnosis, but she had point-blank refused, saying even setting one toe in that place was social suicide. She had made very crass remarks about the sorts of people in there. I know she didn't mean it. Zoe was just so scared of being thought of as a loser, she would do anything she thought would make her more accepted.

I nodded uncertainly.

"Well, that's great!" said Mr Anderson, pulling out a chair. He placed it at the end of his desk and smiled, laying the test and pen on the space in front.

"Now, Ellen, please do not worry if you find this extremely challenging or can't finish the paper. It's just a little quiz so we know which classes will be best for you."

I wish he would just say the word 'test'. I wasn't a child and the word 'quiz' couldn't dull the reality of the fact I could barely answer a single question. Amy and Mr Anderson sat outside, talking in hushed tones as I flicked open the paper. I breathed, scanning the first page, and filling in the answers with ease. Just simple addition, subtracting, division and multiplication sums which I found quite easy from handling the money at home.

Home.

Was that still home?

My heart sank as I turned the next page. More maths...or was it English...as now there were letters mixed into the questions? I turned again and again, feeling myself shrinking to nothing as each problem hit me like a brick. I tried to compose myself as I saw a new section of the booklet - 'English'. I was good at making up stories in my head. I remember countless nights when I had imagined myself in a different world, so vivid I could feel the warmth of the room, the food on the table, a piping hot bath...

I saw a passage of text, about one-and-a-half pages. I tried to read it, but the words danced around like a spider dancing in ink. I concentrated hard, making goggles with my hands to try and focus on the words, but even then they didn't make sense. I tried to remember fleetingly back to my old school days. I remembered how I felt frustrated as I was stuck reading 'Biff and Chip' books while the rest of my class studied proper chapter novels. I remembered how I had special sessions with a lady inside school where I read with coloured plastic over the words.

The C-A-T on the M-A-T.

I managed to distinguish that there was a boy called 'Pirrip', which I thought was a very odd name, and that he seemed depressed. Reading was damn near hard enough, but now there were all kinds of weird-sounding expressions in the text.

I turned the page, salty droplets dampening the paper. They were all questions about the text. I answered as best I could, but was completely stumped after question three. I looked at the clock on Mr Anderson's wall. I had been in here exactly 35 minutes, and I had a whole hour to do the test. I knew attempting any more questions would be useless, so I picked up the test and handed it to Mr Anderson outside the door.

"I'm done," I said, nervously. He looked taken aback, checking his watch.

"Have you checked and double-checked your answers?"

I nodded.

"Have you completed every question?" he asked, sceptically, as he flicked through the empty pages.

Then he looked at my face, seeing I was near tears, and Amy gave him a sideways glance.

"That's wonderful, Ellen, now I will give you and Mrs Brown a tour of the premises."

He went back into his office, placing the test on his desk and putting on his jacket. He took a key out of his pocket and locked the door. I wondered what he had in there that would be so worth stealing?

He gave us both a lanyard to wear, and led us out of the reception. The grounds seemed to eerily quiet to be a school. I imagined all the rows of identical desks with silent pupils under a spell of academia. Mr Anderson took us round the maths classrooms first, then the English. Then he took us round languages and the arts. Languages scared me. I found English hard enough, but now I was expected to learn a whole new vocabulary as well? The only campus that interested me was music. I looked round the classrooms in awe, feeling it was somewhere I could actually understand, running my fingers along the keyboards.

Mr Anderson saw my changed expression and smiled.

"Do you like music, Ellen?"

I shrugged, ducking my head; embarrassed.

"She's just taken up the cello - it was love at first sight," Amy said. "Honestly, she has a very natural musical instinct."

I glowed with pride.

I was slightly alarmed at the science blocks, with their odd chemical smell and actual fire. We went into a Year 9 physics class. As we opened the door, all the pupils' heads raised in interest; otherwise, they all looked bored stiff out of their minds. I saw a girl with wispy black hair and a hunched posture sitting on the back row. She seemed very concentrated on something, which surprised me, because Zoe had always said how much she hated her physics lessons. She looked up and gave me a grin, rolling her eyes at the equations on the board. Then, when Amy was distracted, she held up her work to me. She hadn't been doing physics at all! It was a drawing of us, hugging. She had hatched it with her biro to add amazing depth and expression to our faces. I smiled, happily, so touched that she had drawn it, then quickly dashed over and grabbed it from her. Amy frowned, giving Zoe a warning glance before Mr Anderson led us out of the room. I folded the drawing carefully and slipped it into my jacket pocket.

"Now, Ellen, I'm going to take you to meet your tutor, Mr Macclesfield," Mr Anderson said.

All the way there he continued trying to make conversation with me, asking about my interests or if I had any worries about starting a new school. My answers were mostly monosyllabic or even just head gestures.

He stopped at a chemistry classroom, knocking at the door before opening it. A man was sat behind a computer, his bear-like features intimidating me. He gave a wolfish grin when he saw us, showing a set of bright white teeth.

All the better to eat me with.

"Good morning, Mr Anderson," he said in a booming voice, though there was only us in the quiet room.

He turned to look at me.

"You must be Ellen, Zoe Brown's foster sister?"

I hated the way he said Zoe's name. Tasting the words on his tongue before spitting them out as if they left a vile taste in his mouth.

He pulled out a couple of the seats on the front row.

"Please, sit."

We did as we were told, the man's dominance made clear. No wonder Zoe hated him.

"My name is Mr Macclesfield and I will be your form tutor, Ellen. You will have a 15-minute tutor session in the morning, and another after lunch. In this time, you will do various activities and life skills, such as leadership and career education, as well as catch up on homework and chat to your friends."

I nodded, trying to show interest.

He pulled out a sheet of paper from his drawer. It had students' names lined up in different formations.

"This is my current seating plan for form time," he said, showing us.

There were groups of students bunched together in rows of tables, apart from one student, who was situated alone at the front, with spaces either side of her. I read the name.

Zoe.

"Why is Zoe all alone?" I asked, suddenly feeling anger above my fear.

Mr Macclesfield smiled, icily.

"As I'm sure you're aware, there were a couple of...incidents before Christmas; quite serious. Zoe physically attacked another student, and, as I am sure you understand, when something like that happens, others fear for their safety."

Amy looked slightly upset, but she nodded understandably.

I knew Zoe had scarcely touched that other girl. A couple of scratches at most, and she had far more wounds. Except, hers were invisible.

"Can I sit next to Zoe?" I asked, determinedly.

"Yes, of course," he said curtly, scribbling my name down next to hers. "Though, of course, there are plenty of other nice people in this tutor group."

I forced a smile.

Mr Anderson smiled and stood, looking at his watch.

"Goodbye, Ellen. I hope to see you on Monday."

We all woke early on Monday morning.

I wished it were summer, so I could get up and start the day with a joyful slate instead of a dismal night cloud. I padded along to the bathroom and sloshed cold water over my face and brushed my hair. Amy had laid out my uniform on my chair that we had bought a few weeks ago. I slid each item on slowly, hating the regimented feel of the garments. By the time I got to the tie, I was stumped. Luckily, at that moment, Zoe came into my room and tied the stupid thing for me.

Amy tried to walk with us to school. I wouldn't have minded, but Zoe point-blank refused, saying over and over again that it was social suicide. After a lot of raised voices, Amy sighed, realising she had lost the battle.

"Ellen will be fine, mum. I'll look out for her. It's school where we're going, not a lion's den!"

Except her and I knew it was exactly like a lion's den.

"OK then, but I want no more trouble concerning you at that school, Zoe. I'll see you at one o'clock, Ellen."

She gave us both a hug goodbye, but held me slightly longer and a little tighter than usual, and then watched us to the end of the road.

"Zoe, are you OK?" I asked.

She was walking and texting at the same time, but I could see her face was pale and expressionless. Her eyes were deep pools of stories I wanted to jump into.

"Yeah, I'm fine thanks, Ellen," she said, sliding her phone into her blazer pocket.

"There's just a few rules you need to know."

"Rules?" I asked, confused. "Like not running in the corridors and stuff?"

Zoe laughed, but her eyes did not smile.

"No. You see, Ellen, these rules are sort of...unspoken."

"OK..." I said, starting to get nervous.

"For a start, you have to roll up your skirt," she said, turning to me and rolling her waistband up twice, so it was thigh length.

I didn't understand what was wrong with my skirt the way it was. It now stuck out at an angle and dug into my waist.

Zoe nodded, satisfied.

"Why, Zoe?" I said.

"Just...because. I don't want you to end up like me," she said.

"Now, just stop walking a sec and turn to face me," she said, pulling out a make-up bag.

"No, Zoe," I said, remembering back to her attempted make up in December.

"Look, I've learnt how to do it now. I wear make-up every day, Ellen," she assured me, and pulled out a mascara wand before I could object.

I wasn't sure I liked the feel of the thick black goo on my eyes, scared I would forget and rub them and end up looking like a panda.

She nodded again.

"That's better."

"But, Zoe, I still don't understand. Why do I have to roll up my skirt and wear make-up?"

Zoe stopped and thought for a long, hard few seconds before replying.

"I don't know, Ellen. That's just the way it is. Come on. If we get to school in good time we can sneak into the library before anybody sees us," she said as she strode ahead, a mask of confidence as I scurried behind, terrified of what I'd encounter.

To our surprise, I made friends quickly. I joined most of the music clubs and spent most breaks in the music block, practising. I made friends with several of the girls from the school's orchestra, and the breaks we weren't playing we wandered around in a little group.

Zoe was annoyed when she found out and told me that they were geeks, and making friends would be 'social suicide'.

I was getting fed up of her telling me how I should and shouldn't behave. I knew why, though. She was jealous because she didn't have any friends. Sometimes, I saw her at break, wandering around aimlessly. Sometimes people shouted names at her like 'Retard' or even threw food at her. I watched as she clenched her fists but walked on through as if nothing had happened. I knew why.

Since she had lashed out at Emily in December, everybody had been wary and different in their demeanour towards her.

She was determined to prove that she was 'normal'. I knew my friend gang may not have been high on the social caste system, but we had each other, and the people at the top of the playground didn't seem all that great. Emily seemed all Zoe had described her to be; hourglass figure, long blonde hair, quite intelligent but not a geek. The balance was so perfect it was almost sickening. I saw the way they totally blanked out Zoe, like she really *was* invisible, and the sly pinches under the table. One day, I saw them open her bag and take out a couple of her exercise books. I opened my mouth to tell, but quick as a wink, a girl's hand darted out over mine and she was smiling.

"It's OK, Ellen," she said, like my name was a bitter taste in her mouth.

She then put both hands on my wrist, twisting the skin slowly. My eyes watered.

"You won't tell, will you, Ellen?" said Emily.

I closed my eyes and shook my head, desperate not to cry.

She then took Zoe's exercise books and scribbled on every page in a black Sharpie, sometimes writing things like

'I hate my life' and 'I am so angry'. She then closed the books with a smile, returning them to Zoe's bag.

Zoe had a detention after school that day. She tried to explain it wasn't her, but considering what had gone before, she had nothing to make the teachers believe her.

I saw as she grew hotter and angrier. The more they laid down punishment, the more she protested. I waited outside the door, wanting to burst in and be a witness, but my legs stuck fast.

Weak.

To this day, I still feel a strong sickness of guilt. If only I had stood up for her. But, every time I thought of telling, I pictured Emily's face in my mind, ready to break me. I couldn't afford to be broken any more.

I never took off my school blazer or jumper, even in the sweltering heat, not wanting to expose my scars.

In PE, I always snuck off to get changed in the toilets, and wore joggers and a hoodie. One day, doing running in late June, the PE teacher demanded I remove my hoodie, because my face was flushed to a dangerous level in the summer sun. I tried to protest, saying I liked being warm, but all my excuses were hopeless and feeble. I now had a whole crowd gathered around me, including Emily and her gang.

"She's just as retarded as her sister! Maybe they are related," I heard them snort.

I closed my eyes, knowing I would have to obey the instruction. Slowly, I began peeling off my hoodie, before I suddenly heard a voice shout and come through the crowd.

"Zoe!" I said, relieved, hugging her.

"Let her keep on her jumper," she said coldly to the PE teacher.

The teacher's face was now flushed with anger, her whistle rising and falling with each breath on her big bust, but she controlled herself, and replied, icily: "And why can't Ellen take off her hoodie, Zoe?"

"Because...it makes her feel safe," Zoe said desperately, not wanting to expose my vulnerable past in front of everybody.

"Well, I will have none of that nonsense here. It's nearly 30 degrees! Ellen will boil to death!"

"Please," said Zoe, near to tears.

She was risking another detention just to save me.

"Can we talk over here?" she asked.

The PE teacher reluctantly agreed, and Zoe beckoned me.

"Take your hoodie off, Ellen," Zoe said.

The other students were far away by this point, so, self-consciously, I peeled off my hoodie. The teacher was taken aback and stared, shocked, at my arms.

"Ellen, what are those scars from?!" she asked, peering in sadness at the lines and bumps on my arms.

"What crap this school is!" said Zoe, exasperated.

"Haven't you had paperwork or something?"

Normally, she would have been severely punished for answering back like this, but now, the teacher just shook her head, realising the fault in the system.

"My mum. My mum...it's a long time ago now," I said, tonelessly.

It was in that moment I realised I could never escape the clutches of the past.

Chapter 18

Zoe

I felt so alone.

Isolated.

Like damaged goods that couldn't be returned.

Ava and Emily were friendly enough, and were sickly

sweet in front of the teachers, but any chance of social acceptance was gone. Sometimes they would frame me, doing stupid crimes and saying that I was the culprit. I knew this was revenge, and I knew that when I protested nobody would believe me because I was the crazy one. I couldn't flip out. I had to be normal; innocent. Often, I would have a detention at least once a week.

I drifted around the grounds at break, feeling as if I were naked, as pairs of eyes stared and glared. I had tried to go back to my old group, determined to put the past behind me, though everywhere I moved the truth jabbed me.

Autistic. Autistic. Autistic.

They looked alarmed as they saw me approaching, but Emily smiled at them all reassuringly.

"Just remember what the teachers said, guys. She can't help being mentally unwell, but we can't have our safety jeopardised," she said, gingerly holding up her arm.

"Remember the plan...OK? Just smile and don't engage."

I stopped, feeling as if I was being tangled in a red-hot rope.

"Guys, look, I said I'm sorry. Can we just put everything behind us now?" I said, shaking.

I expected them to come back with a retort or insult, but they all just stood, absolutely silent, with smiles plastered on their faces. It was like they had been possessed and put on pause.

"Guys, I'm talking to you," I said, wobbling.

They all stood, motionless.

"Ava?" I said, desperately looking at my best friend.

She caught my eye for a second, and I felt her guilt. My guilt as well, but then she turned around and walked away, with the others following. I realised then that the friendship that had been hanging by a thread for months had now been cut. And the worst of it was I had been the one to cut it.

By the end of the day, I was nearly in tears. I felt crumpled as I had nobody to hold me up. I told mum when I got home, sobbing into her shoulder.

"It will be OK, Zoe," she said, stroking my back, though I felt as if there were a thousand miles between us.

"But you have to understand, this is your own fault."

I stopped sobbing and stared at her.

My own mum! She was meant to take my side no matter what.

"I mean, you did seriously attack Emily a few weeks ago. You can't blame them for being wary."

"But...mum!"

"Zoe, I know it's hard, but sometimes we have to admit our mistakes. This really isn't the end of the world. Think of Ellen and her life, and you never see that girl make a fuss," mum said, her eyes drifting.

I knew what she was thinking.

Why did she have to have a daughter like me? Why was I such a nightmare when I had nothing to complain about? Why couldn't I make her proud?

"I am so fed up of you always going on and on about stoical little Ellen! So perfect and meek! I see the way you and dad look at her; how you always are so embarrassed of me. I bet you would happily swap us!" I shouted.

Mum looked taken aback.

"Zoe! How dare you speak to me like that. You know that's not true! We love you so much, but we are finding it hard to understand your behaviour at the moment!"

I stormed out of the kitchen, not wanting her to see me break.

As if on cue, Ellen was in the living room on a chair, cello resting on a spike and the bow gliding as dad pointed to music.

I watched as he looked at her. The admiration in his eyes.

Why couldn't I make him proud?

Why wasn't I insanely naturally talented?

"Can't you shut the hell up, Ellen? I'm so fed up of that racket all day! It sounds like a cat clawing," I said.

Ellen looked surprised, but being the perfect angel she was, she didn't retaliate and just sat, twirling her fingers round her bow.

"Zoe, what has got into you?" said dad, his eyes darkening.

I ignored him, turning to Ellen.

"Come on, Ellen, fight back to me! Don't just slump there like a mushroom!"

Ellen sat there, looking deflated. I couldn't take this any more. I ran to my room, calling Sally after me. She followed obediently, padding at my heel. At least somebody loved me. I curled up with her on my carpet and just let myself go. I realised how much I loved Sally, and how she loved me unconditionally. She didn't care. I could go and punch them all in the face a thousand times over and she would still love me. Sally rolled over on to her back and I tickled her tummy, giggling as she pawed me playfully, almost as if she were a puppy again.

Then, I suddenly stopped.

My fingers had run over a bulge in her stomach. My heart was racing. I gently ran my fingers over the same spot again, feeling the lump. It was fairly small, but firm and ominous. As I pressed, Sally suddenly growled and rolled away from me, whining. In over 13 years, Sally had never growled at me. I stroked her, apologetically.

Probably some stupid cyst or something. Loads of dogs get them.

However, as I looked at her again, I saw for the first time the ribs coursing through her fur and remembered how for weeks she had not been finishing her meals. How often after a walk she would get home and vomit. How she looked as if every step was a grinding pain.

I am truly alone.

The next morning, I made mum promise to call the vet. To my anger, she refused, saying she wasn't going to spend hundreds of pounds just for them to check Sally over and say she was fine. However, she did say if Sally continued like this she would take her.

Walking to school, I tried to distract myself, sending funny, filtered snaps back and forth to Ellen. Every time my phone buzzed, I hoped it might be somebody else. I ghosted all the selfies and tags my friends put up and realised how nobody had messaged me for weeks. Not even a 'Merry Christmas' or 'Hey'.

Walking into the grounds that day, and every day after that, it took every inch of my gut not to turn on my heels and bolt. I couldn't. I had to show them I was normal. That the diagnosis was wrong. That it was all a fraud. That they had got the wrong label. That Zoe Brown was a bubbly, popular, typical teenager.

What if I kill Sally?

What if I abuse people?

I have been awful. I am such a bad person.

I punched my forehead, imagining locking up the thoughts in a cast-iron box. It obviously had a broken lock, as seconds later they escaped.

Chapter 19

Ellen

The court case was swift and painful for me.

The actual case lasted for weeks, though I was only there for a matter of hours in total. One day, I arrived and had to state evidence. It stored up so many raw emotions. Every second felt like a sting, but I had to stay numb and emotionless. So much evidence had been given, including awful photos and lots more I was kept away from.

On the last day of the trial, I was led to a room adjacent to the main room and sat in front of a camera and live stream for the final hearing, with Helen and a Witness Service representative for company.

I remember seeing a crazed woman in the dock, screaming. I saw the pure pain in her eyes; the shattered truth before her.

This couldn't be my mum?

My mum was a lovely lady; soft, pretty and loving before it all went wrong.

No! For fuck's sake, Ellen, stop acting like a child.

I hated my mum.

I felt the anger burn and tingle inside me. I wanted revenge. She stole my childhood and murdered my sister.

God help me.

"Not...guilty!" I heard mum gasp.

Not guilty!

Not guilty!

Not fucking guilty!

I wanted to smash through the door, into the dock, and kill her for what she did.

How could she say that when I had literally watched her shake my sister until she DIED?!

"How can you say that, mum! I watched you MURDER her!" I screamed, overwhelmed with hatred and disgust.

"Order! Order!" spoke the judge, glaring.

Helen sat me down. I was shaking with anger. She handed me a glass of water.

I had managed to answer the questions and interrogations truthfully, keeping my eyes closed so I didn't have to see mum and the betrayal in her eyes. I clenched my hands so tightly the knuckles went white, and tears silently seeped down my cheeks. My head was spinning in a torrent of emotion.

After that, there was a short break of nearly a week.

Everywhere I went it was all I could think about, full of anxiety of what the future might hold.

I went back to hear the decision of the jury.

Life sentence.

I screamed as they dragged her away. I tried to run, but they grabbed my arms. I kicked and yelled in agony as my mother disappeared from sight.

I begged them to let me see Mabel one last time to say goodbye, but everyone refused, saying things like, "she isn't in a fit state to be seen; it's better you remember her as she was, alive".

But the last time I remembered her alive was the piercing wails as mum shook her head. Wrenching it back and forth. Back and forth.

The service was short and bitter. I only invited two people: Naomi and Helen. I didn't want the Browns there because this moment was special and sad. A moment for me to say goodbye to the past, without mixing it with the future. I walked up the room with Naomi to find a chair at the front. She was looking around. I could tell she was slightly on edge about something, but she smiled at me sadly and squeezed my hand. I flicked through the order of service, feeling so sad at how bleak and short it was. There were no happy memories to talk about, or achievements in her life. All things that had been snatched away. I traced the flower on the front. Zoe had helped me draw it, carefully defining every petal of a rosebud, forever to remain closed.

I turned around, taking in the empty room, then nearly fell off my seat.

A crazed woman, sitting right at the back of the room, her hands cuffed and chained to a policeman. Her eyes were wild, though her mouth possessed a garish smile.

"Ellen!" she called.

I ran out of my seat, with Helen chasing after me.

"How dare you be here! I hate you. I hate you!" I screamed, clawing at her face whilst Helen pinned my arms...but I was far from finished.

"You disgust me! First you plead not guilty and now you have the nerve to show up to the funeral of my dead sister!"

The woman straightened up, her eyes glazed with medication.

"Ellen, darling, let's all calm down. I am a changed person now. I love you so much and I would never hurt you," she stumbled.

"Have you forgotten? You MURDERED my sister! You fucking murdered her! You're only being kind now because they probably drugged you up to bring you here! I never want to see you again, you pile of shit. I HATE YOU!" I screamed at her, using all the emotion I had, struggling in Helen's grasp.

Words would never be enough to describe the hatred I felt in that moment.

Helen and Naomi pulled me into a side room, screaming. I punched again and again at the hard walls, bloodying my knuckles, needing something, anything to break. I took a mug from the side and hurled it at the floor, feeling the anger explode as it shattered. Then, I almost became disconnected from my body, the emotion sinking, and I just collapsed on the floor in a thousand pieces, sobbing.

For the entirety of the service, I sat, drained of everything, feeling adjacent to my being. I couldn't bear to look back, knowing she would be there, watching.

After the service, I felt so numb I could hardly stand. I watched in silence as the policeman drove away into the distance, with mum clawing at the windows.

The burial was held at a local chapel. I asked for us all to sing 'Twinkle, Twinkle, Little Star' as that was Mabel's favourite song. Mabel deserved so much better, but I gave her all I could. As I watched the miniature wood coffin being lowered into the ground, I thought of everything her life could have been. I imagined me pushing her on a swing, reading her a bedtime story, being there to hear her first word, see her first smile, hear her first laugh. If only I had been a bit quicker. Run a bit faster.

In that moment, I realised just how precious every second of life is, and how life is a venerable gift that can be snatched away at any second. It made me question why there was so much hurt and hatred in life, when all it would take is to make peace.

When her coffin had been completely covered, I knelt down beside the freshly dug earth and let my tears drip on to the soil. I placed down the bouquet of flowers Naomi had bought for me. I had chosen a pink teddy to be in her coffin with her, just like the one I had all those years ago. Naomi had promised she would help me plant daffodil bulbs on her grave for the next spring. The wind was so cold, despite it being March, and the ground was chilled and hard. Mabel would be so cold under all those layers of earth.

Alone.

Forever.

The headstone couldn't be put up for another six months at least, but Helen took me to see it, to see if I liked it. I traced my finger along the writing of the tiny headstone. It was a simplistic design, the cheapest and smallest available, but it was carved with a perfect angel flying in each corner, just as I had asked.

'Mabel Maclaren

23rd July – 27th September

Sorely missed sister'

I felt so broken I just lay on my bed, scared if I moved my body would shatter. Zoe came and lay beside me, holding me close, our tears entwined. She kept telling me I was safe, and she was here if I needed anything. I just kept sobbing uncontrollably, wanting to hurt everybody around me because I was hurting so much, and nobody could understand how I felt. But at the same time, I felt drained of all being.

Zoe went away after a while, leaving me with a glass of water.

"Call me if you need anything, Ellen."

Amy came and sat with me for a while, trying to talk to me, but I just wanted to sink into my own desolate reality.

When Amy had gone, I went back to the wardrobe where I had left Mabel. I brought her out, swaddled in her blanket, and rocked her on my bed, kissing her on her tiny forehead and playing with her fingers. She smiled with her gutless mouth and reached up her hands, pulling on strands of my hair. At least we still had each other, even if mum was gone.

I had been rocking Mabel every day since the court, sharing our sadness, knowing we weren't alone. I stroked her on her tiny, fluffy head, her face creasing up in giggles.

"I love you, Mabel," I whispered, holding her close.

I heard the door open. It was Zoe.

"Ellen?" she said, uncertainly.

I rocked Mabel, protectively. She started crying, so I shushed her, gently.

"It's OK, Mabel, it's only Zoe. She's my other sort of sister."

"Ellen!" Zoe said more forcefully, looking disturbed.

"Look, Zoe, it's my baby sister, Mabel. Isn't she beautiful?" I said, holding her up.

She kicked her tiny legs in exertion.

"Ellen...your sister...don't you remember?!" she said, desperately.

"Remember what? Mum may have been taken away, but we still have each other."

I hugged Mabel tight, feeling her warmth against mine.

"Ellen," Zoe said through a thick voice.

"Your sister is dead. You buried her only a fortnight ago."

"Zoe, don't be silly. She's right here, look!" I said, rocking her.

"Ellen, you're rocking thin air. Ellen...listen to me!"

Suddenly, Mabel's blanket bled scarlet. I screamed as she tumbled to the floor. Falling. Falling.

Dr Mainwaring prescribed me pills called sertraline and these gradually calmed and numbed my poorly head. I felt almost...happy again. I was able to start to enjoy living and the pain gradually eased.

Whilst I was getting better, I couldn't say the same for Zoe. I could tell the level of pain she was in, even if she wouldn't show it. Often, we would watch Netflix series together, arguing over who was the hottest boy, or make fairy cakes in the kitchen and share our future plans.

Recently, though, she has been so tired. She goes to bed as early as 8pm, has dark circles under her eyes as her head throbs, and avoids talking at all costs. She will often randomly go to the park with Sally when she needs to be alone. Sally hasn't been very well for the last few months, either. She walks so much slower nowadays, lifting her paws lethargically as if stepping every movement is sore; her muzzle so faded it is like she has dipped her nose in snow.

Zoe sensed something was wrong. I think she could sense things so strongly; a small breeze was a thunderstorm. At the start, Amy and Tim laughed it off and said 'Sally's just getting older' or 'she probably just ate some grass, stop getting in such a state'. However, I think we could all now see there was something lurking deeper, beneath the surface. There was something even I knew wasn't right about that dog. I could see her ribs sticking through her sides; her black fur sparse and dull.

Everybody was in denial, but I think secretly we all knew the truth. Zoe knuckled her eyes in desperation and fear when Amy said she was going to take Sally to the vets for tests. If nobody speaks of something, you can pretend it's not real and convince yourself of another explanation. When somebody opens your eyes, you have to look the monster straight in the eye.

Chapter 20

Zoe

I could feel it was bad news as soon as I saw their faces.

Walking out of school with Ellen, I was taken aback to see mum and dad waiting for us by the road. They had plastered smiles on their faces, but I could see the tears they had freshly cried.

I froze, the fear hammering at my skull.

Don't let it out.

School was my least favourite place I had to go, other than the therapist's office, and yet, all I wanted to do in that moment was to bolt back into the building. I wanted to do the most aggravating, head-scratching maths paper I could think of! Laugh until my stomach split in two. Feel a thousand silent comments pinned to me as I walked down the corridor. I was about to face one of the worst journeys I would ever have to go on, and I yearned for anything I could to soak up the pain.

"Mum, why are you crying?" I blurted straight out, feeling the words roll off my tongue, with my heart pounding.

Ellen put her arm round me and for once I let her hold me, silently soaking her blazer whilst the school world echoed around me.

"It's gonna be OK, Zoe," she whispered.

I imagined putting a mask on my face, and raised myself, smiling. I couldn't let them see me like this.

Mum rubbed my back, sympathetically.

"Let's pick up an ice cream on the way home!"

The thought of a cool, sweet freshness on my raw, hot throat made me water, and I nodded, however when I was actually licking my lolly, it tasted of cardboard and I disposed of it halfway through.

I tried to walk slowly, dreading the thought of being back in the flat.

Mum and dad were asking all the usual questions about school and life, talking about how much I hated maths and physics, and how Ellen was flying in her music aspects.

I ran straight to Sally's dog basket as soon as I was in the flat, stroking her apologetically.

"Zoe, Ellen, please can you come into the kitchen?"

I walked slowly, placing each foot defiantly, my kneecaps trembling.

"Sit down, girls," said mum, placing two glasses of water in front of us.

"Remember those tests the vet did on Sally a couple of days ago?" said dad, looking at mum, sadly.

Mum stretched out and put her hand on mine.

"Well, unfortunately they came back cancerous."

The room was spinning. I was falling. My world torn apart before my eyes.

"NO!" I screamed, throwing myself on the floor in sheer agony.

I saw tears silently slip down Ellen's cheeks, I think more in sadness for us than for herself.

Thirteen years of love. Thirteen years of trust. Sally had been with me since I was little more than a baby. The only one in the world who didn't judge and who consistently loved me.

Stolen away.

I stopped, defeated, just lying on the floor in between the fragments of my life.

"How long does she have?" Ellen asked, shakily.

"The vet reckons anywhere around 3-8 months. We have chemotherapy tablets for her that will slow it all down and give us more time. They have assured us they will make her overall more comfortable and...not in pain...when the time comes," answered mum.

"Then why can't they make it better?" I shouted in anger.

"They did talk through surgery as an option, Zoe," said dad.

"Then why isn't she having surgery?!"

"Well, Sally is a very old dog, and most likely she would die on the operating table - and even if they did manage to remove it, there are no guarantees, so the vet said it would probably return anyway," dad said, breaking down.

"No...no," I whispered, in despair.

"We're going to make some lovely memories with her in the coming months - and she can hopefully come on holiday to Islay with us one last time in the holidays."

I couldn't take it any more. I ran into my room and cried myself to asleep, exhausted.

Chapter 21

Ellen

June the 28th never used to be a significant date. In fact, we had barely even acknowledged it as far as I could remember, other than it was the biggest mistake of mum's life.

So, this year, I hadn't expected anything different.

In the morning I lay awake in bed, feeling the softness of the duvet around me and the feeling of being safe, telling myself these were the only presents I needed.

I heard giggles and scuffles outside before it all quietened and I received a smart knock on my bedroom door.

"Come in!" I said, grinning.

Amy, Tim and Zoe all filed into my room singing 'Happy Birthday'.

Tim was the only one in tune, whilst Amy hummed, carrying a tray, and Zoe sang with pure happiness but was totally tone deaf.

Amy propped up my pillows and then placed the tray on my knees. Zoe came and slid underneath the other end of the duvet, beaming. On the tray there was a hot chocolate with squirty cream and an array of croissants as a special treat. We all munched cosily in my little room, joking and just simply being happy as one.

Amy, Tim and Zoe handed me two cards, smiling. Amy and Tim's card was very sweet, with a corny music joke of time, saying to have a 'Treb-ly good birthday' with a doodle of music notes. Zoe gave me a look as I opened mine, laughter dancing beneath her eyes. She had spent ages drawing two girls hugging on the front; a similar design to the one she had drawn that day in physics which I kept in the back of my phone case. On the front it said: 'Happy birthday to the best sister in the world'.

Sister.

I gasped as I looked inside, spluttering.

Zoe had drawn Mr Macclesfield, our form tutor, as an angry caricature, holding a megaphone to make a point of his booming voice. Out of the megaphone it said: 'Happy birthday, Ellen, to the whole of London." Zoe had got a very good likeness indeed, exaggerating the dark hairs on his arms and his menacing expression. I looked at her and we burst into laughter.

"What's so funny, girls?" asked Amy, peering over at my card.

"Nothing, nothing...it's just...well, today is so happy!" I spluttered.

Amy and Tim smiled sadly at me.

Today is so happy.

Tim and Amy left me to get dressed while Zoe sat on my bed, swinging her legs, before bringing out a parcel from behind her back.

"Here, I want you to open this now so you can wear it," she smiled, handing me the soft parcel.

I went and sat on the bed beside her, stroking the soft wrapping paper, trying to savour every moment. I wished there was a way you could catch the happy moments and bottle up the feelings to release on a sad day. When I opened the parcel, I found a T-shirt with music notes spiralling around the chest. It fitted perfectly.

"Wow, thank you, Zoe!" I said, grinning as I peered into the mirror.

"No problem," she replied, smiling, leaving me to put the rest of my clothes on.

She insisted on blindfolding me with her hands to walk me to the kitchen table. I stood, transfixed as she took them away. The whole surface was festooned with more parcels and cards, with a '14' balloon bobbing in the air.

I was stunned with newfound joy that I wasn't sure how to express myself for a good 10 seconds, just standing and taking in everything I had missed.

"Thanks," I mumbled, taking a seat.

I opened various cards from aunties and friends whom had obviously heard about my presence, some with a money note or voucher slipped inside. Their messages were often quite awkward and brief, like:

'Dear Ellen,

Happy birthday, with love from Auntie Tina   x
(Tim's sister)'

Them having to explain where they lay on the family tree showed how I would always never quite belong. As I opened each gift, I felt it as their value decreased to me, and whilst I was so grateful for every small token, I realised how they were just objects, and the best thing about that day was the people that surrounded me.

We took Sally to the park and had a picnic. The sun was shining with a still, but not heavy, environment. Sally wagged her tail about us and kept trying to lay on Zoe's lap, oblivious to her size. The only thing that determined she was ill was the fact she wasn't trying to steal any of the food laid out on the picnic rug, unlike her prior Lab behaviour. I think it bothered Zoe, because she kept pressing little titbits of food to her snout, which she accepted, hesitantly. Zoe only picked at her plateful, barely eating anything and chewing for an eternity.

"Zoe, what on earth are you doing?! You've been chewing on that bit of sandwich for about five minutes," laughed Tim, as Zoe forced herself to swallow.

"I have to make sure there's no lumps, so I don't choke," she said, chewing and chewing on minuscule pieces.

"Stop attention-seeking, Zoe," said Amy.

"I'm not," said Zoe, shivering.

She went and hugged Amy.

"I'm just scared of choking, that's all."

"Well, you've never seemed to have had an issue before," she said.

But then...Zoe hadn't been eating with us for the past few weeks, retreating to her room to do 'homework'.

After we had all finished, we continued our amble around the park. Amy and Tim sat down on a bench, but Zoe held me as I went to join them.

"Can me and Ellen go on a walk?" she said.

"Yes, of course, Zoe, but can you guys be back in no more than 10 minutes?"

"Yes, mum," she giggled and pulled me to follow her, Sally panting on her leash a few paces behind us.

"Where are we walking, Zoe?" I asked, as she seemed to expertly weave her way through people and flowerbeds.

"You'll see," she grinned.

She led me to the edge of the park where there were fewer people, where the grass became less regimented and the ground muddier. Zoe looked around then crawled through a weak part in the hedge, which had obviously been used many times before, but she had made sure to curtain it with hedge plant so the entrance stayed exclusive. I crawled after her, afraid of getting my new T-shirt dirty. Zoe then ran along some years of wasteland and into a group of trees.

"Here," she said, sitting down on a log.

I looked around, feeling privileged, as I knew from her face that this was a special place for Zoe. She had hung a dreamcatcher from a nearby branch, and dragged a log into the centre.

"Do you come here a lot?" I asked her.

She played with a stone on the ground, twisting it over and kicking it with her shoe.

"Sometimes, when I need space," she said, lifting her head to look me in the eye. "This is my secret place, Ellen. Nobody knows about it, not even mum or dad. I think it's private land or something, but nobody really cares. I wanted to show you because I always said if I had a best friend I would bring her here, and I suppose you're as close as I'm gonna get."

She grinned at me.

"Wow...it's...nice," I said, looking around at the muddy ground and shabby trees, weeds climbing every surface.

"Look," she said, beckoning to the largest tree in the centre.

She pointed to a name inscribed into the bark, worn in after months of tracing the letters.

'Zoe'.

She handed me some sort of hard metal tool, obviously salvaged from Tim's toolbox.

"You write your name now. It will be faint to begin with, but every time you or I come here, you can go over it again and again until it sticks."

When we returned, Tim and Amy looked a little anxious.

"Ah, did you have a nice walk?" said Amy, giving us each a hug.

"Tim and I have a little extra surprise we thought would be nice to do, seeing as today is such lovely weather."

We walked to the centre of the park to a massive pond. 'Pond' makes you think of some tiny little water hole in your garden, but this pond was so vast and wide it was almost like a lake.

"Wow," I said, staring at the glittering body of silver.

"How would you guys like to have a little boat ride?" said Amy, leading us over to the pedal boat hire.

"Oh yes!" I said, the inner child coming out of me.

"What about Sally?" said Zoe, fondling her ears.

"We can leave her under this tree. She'll probably come in and swim anyway - you know what she's like with water! We'll ask one of the boat hire people just to keep an eye on her," said Tim, sussing it all out.

Zoe didn't look happy, but one look at my excited face and she nodded.

Each pedal boat sat two people, so Zoe and I took one, Tim and Amy another.

"Family deal for four, then?" said the boat hire man, taking the money.

That one sentence meant more to me than that guy would ever know.

Family.

Just the fact that people thought we were a family. That I truly belonged. Pedalling around on that 'lake', I was swelled with happiness. I forgot who I really was. I was one of them. In a family. One of the Browns.

Zoe kept calling Sally to come and swim in the pond, but to her sadness, the old dog stayed, panting under the tree, too tired to move.

Something as silly and childish as pedal boating could bring so much happiness. Ironic that it was this same pond that had brought so much joy, which would also be the one to shatter it.

When we got home later that afternoon, Tim asked that we all sat in the living room. Zoe and Amy gave secret smiles to one another while he was gone, Zoe's hands tingling and flapping as she gabbled how much I was going to love it. Tim returned with an enormous, heavy-looking package that stood almost as tall as me. He dragged it across the floor so it was next to me. He was smiling.

"Here, Ellen. My very good friend was doing up this old one, and it was such a good deal off my chum, we could hardly refuse. You're such a natural at your music already, it's the least we could do," he said.

I gently tore off the paper and opened up the case. My face said it all when I saw it. My very own cello! I flew into Tim's arms and let him hug me tight.

Chapter 22

Zoe

The next few months drifted by in a dulled sadness.

School was the same, except now I had Ellen with me who had gradually increased her days to full-time.

I loved her thinking of me as strong and capable.

I hated her seeing me at school. Weak and alone.

I couldn't help but feel jealous. To my surprise, Ellen made friends quickly. Joining most of the music clubs, she found herself in this slightly geeky group of girls. They may not have been socially high in ranking, but they had each other, which shielded them. The music department soon took a shine to her and asked her to perform in several things in the end-of-year show.

"She's scarcely been playing six months and she's already so good," I spat to mum that evening.

"Well isn't that lovely for her, Zoe? She's really struggling in all other aspects of school life," Mum said, icily.

I suppose she was right.

Poor Ellen apparently had the school knowledge of a nine- or 10-year-old for her maths, and even lower in her sciences. I had heard mum and dad discussing how she could barely read. The school had decided to give her a dyslexia test, in which she came out as severely dyslexic. She had to have extra coaching for these lessons in place of what would have been her French lessons, but the school thought trying to learn a language at this stage would be too difficult 'given the situation'.

I often wished I had the power to be invisible and to escape. I always felt eyes bore into me and the hundreds of silent thoughts.

At this point, I didn't know what OCD was, or how it was consuming my life, but every day the words got stronger and stronger. Often, I could no longer tell what accusations were real and which ones had been forged by my brain. Every day, I just felt so increasingly alone. I watched the gaggles of friends so trusting and happy with one another and realised how empty I felt. I couldn't sit down at breaks, as sitting alone without friends made you a target at the best of times, so I would wander around with my hearty load of anxiety, feeling as if I were Mary and all the inns were full.

The medication had shrunk Sally's tumour and she got a newfound life. I watched as she regained the spring in her step and wagged her tail more and more. I began to gain a sense of childish hope that Sally was getting better, even though I knew deep down it was only the medication. It was like how I could convince myself that the psychiatrist had got the diagnosis wrong. I mean, they had hardly talked to me for goodness' sake, but again, deep down of course, I knew it was true.

The summer holidays came as a welcome relief from the day-to-day drain of school. I loved the feeling of being able to go to sleep without the niggle of tomorrow's test or homework I needed to complete, what I would do at break, or how I literally had no friends and didn't know how to make any as I had quite frankly screwed up my reputation.

Every summer, we went to stay on the island of Islay in a little weathered cottage left to dad by an old aunt. It was almost on the seafront, so picturesque that it looked like part of a dream. It only had one proper bedroom and was quite small and cosy. I had grown to love the little cottage, with the little fishermen's yard and salt-stained window panes. It was so peaceful. The only thing that slightly unnerved me was the thought of discovering a ghostly old aunt drifting around the attic of her old realm.

This year would be different though, as we would have Ellen. Over the past 10 months, I had grown rather fond of her, but I still wavered about the thought of sharing something so special within the family with her.

On Sunday morning we started the tedious journey; the whirring and buzz of the motorways in tune with the hum of questions in my head. With nothing to focus on, they soon became so strong it felt like there was screaming in my head and I clutched it, near to tears.

Mum looked at me via the car mirror.

"Zoe, are you alright? You don't feel travel sick, do you?" she said, turning round to peer at me.

Ellen slid off her headphones and looked at me, anxiously.

"No, I'm fine, mum. I don't feel sick," I said, forcing a smile, though the ringing was still whirring.

You're a bad person.

You have abused Ellen.

What if I wish that mum was dead?

"Then why were you clutching your head like that?" Mum asked, confused.

I stopped, heart beating, wondering how on earth I was supposed to explain.

"Mum...do you ever get...like questions and statements in your head...like a voice telling you stuff and even though super deep down you know it's not true, they kind of convince you that you've done loads of awful things?" I said quickly, feeling blood rush to my cheeks.

Mum thought, looking very worried.

"Are you hearing voices in your head, Zoe?" she asked, sadly.

"No, not like that. It's kinda more like...I don't know...silent thoughts, except, they're so loud they kind of take over sometimes," I said, feeling stupid. "Sorry, that sounds daft. Please, let's not talk about it any more."

Ellen gave me a hug and offered me a sweet.

Mum looked at dad in adult code of '*I am worried our daughter has completely lost it.*'

After a whole day of driving, we finally arrived in Kennacraig, where we stayed the night in a hotel before getting a ferry across to Islay.

"You'll never guess what the ferry port is called!" said dad in astonishment, checking crossing times on his phone. "Port Ellen!"

"Are you serious?" said Ellen, laughing.

"Maybe they named it after me!"

"It's almost like it was meant to be," said mum, joining dad and gazing at Ellen in wonder as if an angel had descended from heaven. Of course, I was the screwed-up devil!

I wasn't at all happy about leaving poor Sally in the car, especially in her current condition. She looked at us in betrayal as we got out of the vehicle. I insisted on filling up her water with a freshly chilled bottle and leaving all the windows slightly open for fresh air.

"Come on Zoe, Sally will be fine. We are on the boat just a couple of hours!" said mum, trying to pull me away as cars were piling in behind us.

My eyes watered as Sally whined in the boot. I knew she would be fine, and that we would all be back together in a couple of hours, but I couldn't help but wonder if it would be the last time I saw her. Sally could suddenly have a bad turn and die in the car while we were gone.

By the time we reached the cottage, it was early afternoon, and we were all exhausted. Dad went to lie down upstairs, complaining of a migraine coming on from the long drive.

I showed Ellen to my room. It was a tiny, cosy box room in the attic. Mum had left fresh sheets on the one bed, which filled almost half of the room. I had hung fairy lights across the beams and dad had fixed a little window with a hatch. There were still rows of shells laid out on the chest of drawers from last year. I stroked them, trying to go back.

So much had changed in the space of one year. This time last year I felt so light, so normal, with no rocks in my head. Ava was my best friend, and we texted every day. Sally was a perfectly healthy dog, with only a few grey hairs.

Mum came into the room, laden with a blow-up mattress and more bedding, laying them down.

"Now, at the moment, there is only one proper bed in this room, though of course we plan to change that in the future," she said.

"I think the only fair thing we can do is toss a coin, girls."

I stopped, rigid.

This was *my* holiday.

The one time in the whole year where I actually could rest and have fun - and now I might not even have a proper bed!

My face grew hot as I thought about the dips and squishiness of the blow-up mattress sliding around beneath me.

"Oh, Amy, if Zoe doesn't mind then please can I have the blow-up? It would be just like camping!"

I looked at her.

Ellen looked straight back at me, smiling.

I hoped she was being genuine and not just helping me. To this day, she is still the most selfless person I know.

That holiday consisted of many happy memories. However, for those couple of weeks, I carried around guilt, because I hated how the precious good times were spoilt by my obsessive thinking.

One day, when we went for a cliff walk, I was near tears as my head kept telling me again and again that I had abused Ellen. I knew it wasn't true...was it?

You are a bad person.

You touched her.

Remember when you hit her on the arm? That's abuse.

All this time, I almost forgot that Sally was dying. Though she walked a little slower and chose to lay down on the beach instead of swim, she was no longer throwing up her food or crying with pain. Normally, being a Labrador, Sally's favourite thing about our holiday was swimming in the sea. She would stay in there for what seemed like hours as I repeatedly threw a tennis ball into the waves for her to fetch. Often, she would puncture a hole in the tennis ball so it sank, and consequently refused to get out until she had found it or something to replace it, like a piece of driftwood. Now, however, she refused to go near the water, looking at me sadly and soulfully when I tried to pull her in. Every day at the beach she would just lie on a nest of sand and sleep.

Despite going to Islay every year, I still wasn't a good swimmer. In fact, I could hardly swim at all and made sure to stay well in my depth.

One day, I was kicking mindlessly on my bodyboard when I couldn't control the thoughts any longer.

What if you wish for your parents to die?

I wish that my-

No!

What if you say it and they die, and it's all your fault?

NO!

I smacked my head, hard.

I tried to distract myself, but I was too swallowed up in a nightmare of convictions.

I wish that my parents were dead.

No, I didn't mean it.

What if they drop dead now?

207

I think it is very hard to imagine what OCD thinking is like if you have never experienced it. It's like being controlled and manipulated into believing and saying awful things about precious things such as your family. Except...the only monster is living and breathing inside you. Because the bully *is* you.

I had become so engaged in the knot of torment, I hadn't noticed myself drifting further and further away from the shore. I tried to put my feet down and panicked when I failed to feel the bottom. I looked around me and could see nobody. Mum was asleep like a dot on the beach, and dad and Ellen had gone for a walk. I saw other figures on the beach and some people paddling further down. I didn't want to call out. I couldn't be more of an embarrassment to mum and dad. I couldn't behave like a child. Just be normal, Zoe.

At that moment, a strong wave tipped me off my board. I struggled in the water, feeling it burn and gush up my nose. I thought of Ashwood Forest residential, almost a year ago now, and how I had slipped under the boat. It had been under 10 seconds before people hauled me out.

But...there was nobody here. Nobody to tell me I was too quiet, too ugly, too outspoken. There were no voices slyly hissing, nor the permanent silent scroll of social conduct. There was no silent embarrassment and disappointment.

Somehow, down here, the ocean just let me breathe, even though I could feel the burning in my lungs.

But...no, I could do it. I could stay just a little bit longer this time. Just to escape for a little bit...

I heard hysterical shouting.

"Zoe! Zoe!"

No. Just stay a little bit longer. Don't let the outside world in just yet. But I felt dad's hands grip me and haul me out. I automatically gasped for air, coughing. He put me on my bodyboard and swam me to the shore.

To my surprise, it wasn't long before dad could stand, and I realised I hadn't been that far out at all.

"Zoe, what the heck were you doing?!"

"Just...swimming," I shrugged, shaking.

"How dare you give us all such a scare! You know you can't swim! Poor Ellen is crying - she thought you were dead!" said dad.

I darkened.

"Poor Ellen. It's always about *poor* Ellen. Little, saintly, goddamn Ellen...so perfect!" I sobbed.

I didn't hate Ellen at all. In fact, I was growing to almost love her. I just felt bitter. I felt so lost and hurt, and mum and dad *couldn't* understand.

In the last few days of the second week, Sally began pulling on her lead whenever we took her out for a walk, or she'd simply lay down, there and then, and be sick again.

Even I had to admit that there could be no more lies. The end was approaching.

Only a couple of days after we had returned, all the magic of the fortnight faded. When we took Sally for her usual amble at the park on Thursday morning, she limped into the bracken and lay down amongst the green fronds. I called her, but she didn't return. I went and tried to pull her up by her collar, but her whimpers broke my heart. I screamed for mum, and she came wading through the bracken.

"Oh, Sally," she said sadly, fondling her ears, before hugging me tight.

My lips wobbled as I tried to hold myself in, hugging Sally's body tight. Dad groaned as he lifted Sally up and put her over his shoulder, using all his strength. He carried her to the car, all the time Ellen mumbling to me that 'it was going to be OK'. Except, it wasn't. Nothing would ever be OK again. Dad laid her heavy Labrador body in the boot, stroking her back.

"We need to call the vet!" I said desperately, trying to have some - any – form of useless hope.

"Yes, Zoe, I will call the vet when I get home," said mum, squeezing my hand.

I was flooded with a split second of light before reality hit me.

"No, mum! Not yet!" I sobbed, bitterly.

"Sally is in so much pain, Zoe. She can barely walk any more. It's much kinder to let her go."

Dad laid Sally on her dog bed at home while mum called the vet. Naomi turned up about half an hour later to subtly take Ellen out of the equation for a few hours.

I rounded up all of Sally's favourite dog toys and balls, tucking in all of her blankets around her. I stroked her and whispered all of our memories, right back to when I found it hazy to remember.

I didn't move, even when I heard the doorbell ring and the vet come in.

I wanted to stop life. Stop time.

But all too quickly we were there, surrounding Sally's dog bed. I sobbed uncontrollably as the vet deftly slid the needle into Sally's leg, having a crazy urge to rip it out. Sally looked at me with her deep, dark, brown eyes, with such a surreal sense of peace I could feel it wave through me. I bent down and kissed her dry nose.

"Go and swim in the stars, Sally. I love you."

And then she let out a deep sigh and fell still.

Chapter 23

Ellen

When Naomi dropped me back at Zoe's house in the early evening on Thursday, I could hear muffled sobs coming from inside.

I ran inside and pushed past Amy and Tim to the landing. I found Zoe there, curled up in Sally's dog basket, tears pouring down her wet cheeks. I knelt down beside her.

I knew I mustn't touch, though I reached out and tentatively stroked Sally's head. The fur was grey and worn; her body was lifeless.

I didn't bother building Zoe up with false promises. Sometimes, you just have to be real.

"I know right now must feel extremely hard for you Zoe," I said very softly.

Zoe carried on sobbing hysterically.

"I HATE YOU! I HATE YOU!" Zoe screamed at the sky, the words scratchy and thick.

Then she sniffed.

"I want her back!"

"I know, Zoe."

"How would you know?" she spat.

I couldn't hide from the past any more. This time I let the memories that I had buried cascade over me, taking control.

"I understand, Zoe, because the same happened to me," I whispered.

I thought it would be agony, talking about Mabel and mum again. I could just forget, but pushing down your scars doesn't get rid of them. The wound is still there under the plaster.

"It still hurts a lot, Zoe, I can't deny it," I said after a while.

"And does the pain ever stop?" Zoe spluttered.

"No. But with time it gets a bit better, and every night I look out of my window at the stars, and I think maybe, just maybe, Mabel is up there, looking down on us."

"But how will I survive, Ellen? Sally was my whole world and now she's gone," she said bitterly. "I'm completely alone."

I laid my hand gently on her shoulder, and she didn't protest.

"I know you don't want to say goodbye, Zoe. Nobody does. I am here for you."

"Goodbye, Sally," she whispered. "I love you."

Zoe let me lead her from the landing, before she collapsed onto her bed. I knew she had no tears left to cry, nor the strength to feel anything but bitter sadness. Sally was so intertwined in her heart that it was now shattered.

They had Sally cremated and laid the small urn on the mantelpiece. It made me feel strange, looking at them, thinking Sally was actually in there, just grey dust that had only been living and breathing a few weeks ago.

Zoe had a small portion of the ashes made into a necklace, which she wore all the time, close to her heart. She didn't want to decide what to do with the rest just yet. Zoe seemed constantly distant. She seemed to have lost all her sparkle.

Chapter 24

Zoe

I felt as if nobody could ever understand. I yearned for the time when I was so young, and the biggest worry I had was a whisper about nothing, instead of a continuous scream about everything.

For a while, Sally's dog bed lay on the landing as a bitter carcass of remaining light I could never retrieve. Dad ended up moving it under their bed, just so I didn't have to look at it any longer.

As the months went by, I grew ever more isolated.

The new school year was no different, either. Now in Year 10, the teachers piled on work for our GCSEs. I almost liked doing the work because it gave me a reason to think. Think about anything, because if I didn't, then those menacing thoughts would come.

At night, I put headphones on and blared music into my ears until I fell asleep, just to keep the thoughts away. I knew mum and dad loved me, but they couldn't understand me. Nobody could.

It was almost like a full circle when it came to October and all of our geography class were invited on a field trip residential to the South Downs. I thought of the

Ashwood Forest residential over a year ago, and cringed at my past self. So scared, so open, so desperate for attention. While I still felt a gnawing nervousness of staying a night away, it was more an annoyance than an extreme fear.

We set off on a dreary Tuesday morning. Thankfully, Mr Macclesfield wasn't present; instead, it was three of the geography staff and a couple of teaching assistants. I sat, slouched against the window, not expecting anybody to sit by me. To my surprise, I then felt somebody sit in the seat next to me. I turned to see the face of long-ago happiness and friendship.

"Ava?" I said, shocked.

She smiled awkwardly.

"Hey, Zoe."

"What are you doing here?" I said, bluntly.

We had literally not spoken for over half a year. She was just a figure of my past.

"Well...we were best friends, weren't we?" she said, holding out her hand in the start of our childhood handshake.

Suddenly, I was filled with a burst of joy as I realised maybe I wasn't so alone.

All that long coach journey, it was just like the old days. We laughed, chatted, played stupid games and talked primary school memories. I felt my insides go warm and fuzzy with the feeling of friendship. It was almost as if nothing had happened, and we had gone back in time. She never apologised, but I was so desperate for friendship I didn't bring up the past months.

I couldn't help but look around for Emily. She was sitting further back with a bunch of my old friendship group. She caught my eye and glared. I could sense tension in the air.

When we got off the coach for a toilet break at a service station, I heard Emily and Ava having a hushed argument.

"Ava, why are you hanging out with that freak again? I thought we agreed she's a nightmare and we don't want to be associated?"

"I know...but, she kinda seems sad, and I don't know...maybe she has troubles of her own. Maybe she deserves a second chance?"

"Well, I tell you one thing. It's me or the freak!" Emily said before storming off.

For the second part of the journey, Ava was a lot more subdued, answering with monosyllabic sentences or a shrug, and kept peering back nervously at Emily. I tried bringing up more of our primary school memories, like the time we went to the lido together for my 10th birthday, and Ava ate so much ice cream and chips she had to get out of the car and be sick on the long journey home.

"Shut up, Zoe," she said lightly enough, but I could feel the edge to her voice.

I bristled.

"You don't have to feel sorry for me, Ava. Go sit over there with Emily and the rest of the orange-skinned *cool* people. Don't feel you have to be friendly."

Ava feebly protested, but then fell silent for the rest of the journey, tapping away on her phone.

I wished Ellen were here, but she hadn't taken geography as an option.

When we arrived, it was just before noon, and we sat to have lunch on some random grassland. I looked around awkwardly, wondering where I should sit. Were me and Ava friends now? She was looking awkward too, looking over at her friendship group and then at me. Then, she smiled and beckoned me to join her. We sat and ate sandwiches and crisps in silence, every now and again awkwardly catching each other's eye.

Ava swallowed.

"I heard about Sally. I'm sorry," she mumbled.

"Thanks," I said, trying not to engage emotionally, ripping up grass with my fingers.

"Erm...would you like to share a room with me?" she said, smiling.

I forgot all about trying to play it cool.

"Oh yes! We can make Tik-Toks," I said, trying to be cool.

Ava laughed.

"You're such a child, Zoe. You don't even have Tik-Tok."

I always felt I couldn't win. If I talked about weird stuff, I was too boring. Apparently, if I tried to be like them, I was childish.

After lunch, we travelled to some chalk hills and had to take some boring studies on the slope formation and rock - most of which I didn't pay attention to.

We then went back to some sort of youth hostel. As promised, Ava shared a room with me. We were told to hang out in the dining room until we got served tea. Ava pulled me over to Emily and all my old gang. They hushed up and glared at us approaching.

"I thought we had a deal, Ava?" said Emily, eyebrows raised.

"Yeah, but you're being a bitch, Emily!" said Ava, annoyed.

There was a pause as Emily took in what Ava had said. Then, she very calmly, very slowly, spoke.

"*I* am the bitch?"

Ava swallowed and looked away.

"That's what I thought," said Emily.

"Look, Emily, just let them sit with us," spoke a voice.

It was James - the guy who I had once sat next to in maths and had good, fun banter with. The boy who I had flipped out at all that time ago and had never spoken to since.

I looked up and caught his eye, a thousand unspoken words between us.

I'm sorry, you were right. I am autistic.

"And you can keep your opinions quiet too James, or you can go and join the retarded group," Emily said, but I could sense her fear. Her fear of losing power.

"Fine then. Be like that," snapped Ava, pulling me back.

"Come on, Zoe. Let's go to our room."

For about half an hour we tried to have fun in our bedroom. There were actually five single beds lined up in it, but thankfully a few people had dropped out last minute thanks to winter bugs, so there was leeway on space. We tried to crack jokes and have fun, but we both knew there was something between us now.

My phone buzzed. It was Ellen.

She sent me a snap of her and mum, with **'How's it going? xx'** as the caption.

I didn't want her to worry about me. I didn't want mum to think I was an attention-seeker. I snapped back with a selfie of me and Ava. **'Really good, ty. Just hanging with Ava before tea xx'**

She replied instantly. **'Ava? Isn't she the one who excluded you from her birthday then framed you?! xxx'**

I switched off my phone, not wanting to think about the past.

"Erm...hey, we should probably get down for dinner," said Ava.

We made queues at two tables with teachers serving at a makeshift pasta bar.

I knew I couldn't eat without being sick. When it was my turn, I just had a spoonful of plain pasta and a glass of water.

I sat down at a table and waited for Ava to join me. She came over, looking kind of awkward.

"Hey, Zoe, I'm just going to sit with Emily for tea if that's OK?"

She didn't wait for a reply and hurried off. It was obvious I wasn't invited. So, I was back to being a loser after those six hours of reignited friendship. I took a mouthful of pasta and chewed.

Don't swallow, Zoe.

There might be lumps.

You could choke.

I knew it was nonsense. I couldn't listen to the voices. But I seemed to have forgotten how to swallow.

What if you are sick?

What if mum drops dead while you're away and it's all your fault because you wished for her to die?

Wish for mum to die!

Wish it!

I shook my head. I couldn't let the thoughts in. Not now.

Slowly and forcefully, I managed to swallow the mouthful of pasta and chucked the rest in the bin.

I slipped off to my room, not seeing a need to stay any longer; not wanting to stay any longer.

I realised I was exhausted from emotion and just simply drained of energy. I had a quick wash in the shared shower space and then got into bed. I was tired but I couldn't sleep.

I could hear laughing downstairs. I had to focus on that. Focus on something other than the silence. I put my headphones on and belted my music playlist into my brain to flush out the thoughts. I went to sleep that night, reminded again of who I was.

The next morning, I woke early and turned in my bed to see Ava still asleep in the bed next to the window. I checked the time. 6.43am. I knew we had to be down for breakfast by 8. I crept over to Ava's bed and just stood over her, watching her breathing and remembering who she used to be. Who I used to be. What life used to be.

I went along the corridor to splash my face with water and use the toilet. When I returned, Ava was awake, getting dressed.

"Morning, Ava," I said.

"Morning, Zoe," she replied, sleepily.

"How was last night?" I asked with a slight edge.

"Fine, thanks," she said quickly, not looking me in the eye.

"You excited for rock studies today?" I said sarcastically.

"Absolutely ecstatic!" replied Ava with equal sarcasm.

I got dressed quickly and walked down to the hall with Ava. To my surprise, she led me over to my old friendship group to eat breakfast. I thought I would get the same, cold greeting as yesterday, but they all grinned at me and sat me down like nothing had happened. At first, conversation was awkward, but soon it eased into the old times, and I felt truly as if I belonged. If only that was really the case.

After a dreary morning of studying rocks and identifying weathering impacts, my brain was more weathered with boredom than the case study.

We had packed up our bags that morning and were having to lug them around on our backs. I was glad the weather was chilled, or I would've boiled.

223

As I look back, I cringe at myself for being too trusting of those girls.

Before we got on the coach, we were told we could spend our money in the souvenir shop or buy sweets for the journey. Though why anybody would want a souvenir of some rock I don't know!

Ava suddenly gave a shocked cry as she stood next to me and opened her purse.

"I...don't understand," she said, feeling in her bag. "I packed £20 in my purse. I know I did," she stated, getting het up.

"Oh no!" I said, putting my arm around her. "It'll be OK, Ava. I'll help you find it - and if we can't, you can have half of my money," I said, hating to see her upset.

Upon hearing the disturbance, one of the teachers came over and asked what was going on.

"All my money has just...gone," said Ava, showing her the empty purse.

"Are you sure it has not just slipped out into your bag?" the teacher asked.

Ava nodded. "I've checked twice."

"And how much was in there?"

"Twenty pounds altogether; a £10 note and two £5 notes," she fretted.

"Who were you in a room with last night?" asked the teacher.

My heart thumped.

"Zoe," said Ava, nodding to me. "But she would never do a thing like that, Mrs Smyth. Zoe's my best friend in all the world," Ava said as she hugged me, smiling.

The teacher grabbed my bag all the same. I was irritated that she was violating my privacy for something I knew I hadn't done, but I didn't worry too much as I had nothing to hide.

Emily had sidled over at this point, comforting Ava.

"Look, it's fine, Ava. I'll buy you some sweets and a souvenir, and whatever," she said, hugging her.

Mrs Smyth was delving into the front pocket of my rucksack by now. I stopped as she pulled out several notes from the pocket.

20 pounds. Oh shit!

"Zoe...?" Ava said, staring at me in anger. "I thought we were friends now?! I thought you were a different person! I should've known," she said, pulling away from me to Emily.

"How could you after we welcomed you back to the group after everything?!" spat Emily.

"Guys! I didn't take the money...!" I started.

Mrs Smyth scowled at me and handed Ava the money.

"Zoe Brown, care to explain this?" she said, sharply.

"I didn't take the money, I swear! Ava is my best friend!"

I pleaded. Hopelessly.

I was excluded for three days from the moment we got back to school. Mum didn't look angry when she picked me up. More confused and emotionless.

"Mum, I swear I never took the money!" I said, the moment she walked into reception where Mr Anderson, the headmaster, and a member of admin were waiting with me.

Mum took a deep breath in and nodded.

"I just need time to process this, Zoe," she said, flatly.

"No, please! Believe me! I would never do a spiteful thing like that. Why do you believe them and not me?"

Mr Anderson sighed deeply.

"Unfortunately, due to your past with this group of girls involving the physical attack on Emily, we have strong evidence to take their side in this situation."

"But I would never do a thing like that! I wouldn't just hurt my friend for no reason!" I said, angrily.

"What about the incident that happened last December?"

Because they baited me. They wanted me to lash out. They hurt me far more than I hurt them, but you can't see that because words don't leave physical scars.

I slumped and ducked my head, realising I was defeated. At that moment, the door opened, and Ellen walked in.

"Oh, Zoe, I heard what happened! I know you would never do a thing like that!" she said, rushing over to hug me.

Mr Anderson sighed and sat back on his chair.

"Ellen, why are you out of class?" Mr Anderson asked.

"Because I am tired of covering everything up for those *bitches*!" she said, angrily.

"Language!" Mr Anderson cut in sharply.

"Those girls set her up, Sir, they are nothing but nasty. Tell them, Zoe," she begged me.

All this time, mum was just staring in disbelief at the scene unfolding in front of her.

"Tell me what?" said Mr Anderson.

"Nothing, Sir," I said, glaring at Ellen, who wouldn't be quiet.

"They repeatedly call her horrid names. Ava, her best friend, excluded her from her birthday party and set it up to record Zoe behind McDonald's that day!" she exploded.

"That's quite an accusation, Ellen, with no evidence," said Mr Anderson.

"Not inviting somebody to a celebration and name-calling are very different to physical attacking and theft."

"But...Sir...you have to believe me!" said Ellen.

"If I may, Mr Anderson," started mum, still in shock. "I know my daughter well. She can make stupid decisions when provoked, but she would *never* do a thing like that."

Mr Anderson breathed in deeply.

"OK. I will take this new information into consideration. Have you got any evidence?"

I thought.

The messages? No. My texts had been angry and bitter on the spur of desperation.

"Her exercise books!" said Ellen. "The other day, Emily took them out of Zoe's bag and scribbled on the pages and wrote stuff. Zoe got detention for it, even though it was never her."

"And how do you know it was Emily?"

"Because...because I watched her do it," she said.

I stared at her. Ellen, the one person in the world who I had put trust into had betrayed me and weakened like all the rest. I caught her eye, and her eyes glazed as she saw she had broken the bond of our trust.

"And why didn't you say anything at the time?"

"Because…I was scared of Emily," she mumbled.

"Right. I'm afraid now your evidence is weak, and though I will take this into consideration, five students have written statements for why they think Zoe stole the money. They even said she left the hall early to go to the room," he said.

I couldn't bear to look at Ellen as mum and I walked out of the reception, trampled.

I wanted to run home and curl up with Sally in her dog bed, but Sally was fucking dead.

Dead like my life and dead like my friends.

My gerbils were cute and funny, but the little balls of fur were hardly the same as a big, strong, emotionally engaged dog.

So I ran. I ran to the only place I could. My secret place. I clawed and kicked at the tree in which Ellen and I had inscribed our names so lovingly on that happy day in what seemed like another life. I ran out, the cold breeze lifting me away from reality. I found myself next to the pond, on which we had gone boating last summer. All the pedal boats were in storage now as it was approaching winter. The wind created a ripple effect on the surface of the pond. I stared down at my reflection and saw a thousand pieces of myself staring back in each wave. A thousand things I could've been.

If only I wasn't Zoe.

Chapter 25

Ellen

Even after the suspension, Zoe refused to go to school for nearly a week. She just lay in bed each morning, utterly refusing to get out until she knew it was too late to go to school.

I went to school on the Thursday after it had happened. I couldn't contain my anger. I had to prove to Zoe that I cared. I marched up to the group of girls, they turned to me in a wall as I approached, giving sideways smirks and chewing on their gum.

"You bitches!" I spat. "I know what you did."

Emily smiled, raising her eyebrows.

"I am so sorry you feel this way, Ellen. I am sorry you think me the bitch in this situation," she said, smoothly.

I looked at Ava. She could only look me in the eye for one second, before she looked away.

"Your sister physically attacked me last year and stole money from Ava out of sheer spite. She has called us horrible names, anything we have said back was entirely in self-defence," she said, as if she had it all planned out.

Amy forced Zoe to go back into school the following Wednesday, physically dragging her out of bed. To my surprise, Zoe didn't protest.

Over the next couple of months, I watched as she slowly shrunk into herself, until one day, she became silent. She was too tired to talk to herself. I never realised she was constantly fighting her own battle every second of each day. It went on like this until that Christmas Day, when she finally broke. She simply lay in a ball in the corner of the room for hours, wishing to us all that she could die.

If only I had known then.

Maybe I could have stopped her.

Chapter 26

Zoe

I couldn't do this. I hated myself.

I hated the essence of life.

I hated autism.

I didn't want to live any more. I had lost my best friend in all the world. Forever.

Living, without a life. A constant swirling mess of a brain, screwed up and controlled by anxiety. I couldn't live.

People say words cannot hurt you.

In my experience, words can hurt so much more than any broken bone, any burn or any cut.

Just one word can instantly destroy you in all of those ways, but you cannot bandage your wounds because you are the only one who can see the pain.

I felt broken. Shattered into fragments. My head was a whirling mess of rebounding OCD that I had no power over. I often woke up in the night, screaming internally as the thoughts attacked me constantly. I would ram on my headphones, turning up the music to full volume, clawing at my head. Nothing could block them out.

I refused to eat, only sipping water. I didn't want to live. I remembered those words that Emily had said to me; dark and yet so right.

'Why don't you go and kill yourself? Nobody would care, because you're a freak and a loser!'

She was right. She was right.

FREAK.

Why don't you just go and kill yourself?

Nobody would care.

Kill yourself.

Kill yourself.

A sudden memory hit my head. The residential at the beginning of Year 9.

The unforgiving anxiety. Being pushed off the boat, finding peace in the water under the kayak. Drowning.

Last summer being swept out to sea. Finding solace.

Peace and pain merging into one.

I knew what I needed to do.

Rummaging in my drawer, I tore out a page of my notebook and scribbled hurriedly.

My heart pounded under my school shirt. Then, with feet aching and arms flapping, I ran.

I knew the way.

It was January, yet my forehead was drowning in sweat.

Drown.

Drown.

The trees were bare and stripped of their leaves, frost lacing every twig and branch in an eerie blanket of white. I thought of mum, dad and Ellen.

Oh God!

Why are you doing this?

Shit, Zoe!

I felt a cold wind blow into my face, and enabled the thoughts to stab my brain.

What if I kill my family?

What if I abuse people?

I'm a danger to society.

What if I'm sick?

You abused Ellen, Zoe.

You're the reason Sally died. You wished it to happen.

Punish yourself.

'You're a FREAK, Zoe.'

'I didn't invite you, because you're a FREAK.'

'Loser.'

'Nobody likes you.'

'You're a FREAK.'

'Why don't you go and kill yourself? Nobody would care...'

Kill yourself.

Kill yourself.

The grass was frosty beneath my school shoes, every blade crunching in protest as I ran frantically across them. I ran across the park. Every puffed breath of air reminding me I was *alive*.

I stared down at my reflection in the ice of the pond where we had gone boating. I didn't see Zoe Brown. I saw a *FREAK*; a girl nobody wanted as their friend. A sad nobody.

'Why don't you go and kill yourself? Nobody would care...'

Kill yourself.

Kill yourself.

I tipped back my head and screamed. A scream vast and wide. A scream that bellowed out every pain and agony of the past month. My past *life*. A scream that I thought would end me, forever. I was free.

I stared at my phone. Every message a stab to the chest, reminding me of who I was. I hurled it onto the ice.

For a moment, I just stared as the surface cracked.

I thought...

...then I jumped, feeling my legs buckle and break the ice, my heart stabbed of breath.

I couldn't breathe. I mustn't think. I felt free.

Freedom at last.

I felt my lungs tighten and my skin be attacked by the sheer reality of life.

Hold on, Zoe.

I shut my eyes. Closed myself. Just a body under ice.

Every broken piece of me was healed. The shattered pieces of my past, mended. I was calm. I was free. The pain would soon be over.

Let yourself be taken, Zoe.

Let it take you.

And I let darkness swallow me up.

Handler: "Emergency, which service do you require?"

Caller [hysterical]: "Ambulance! Oh God, please come quickly!"

Handler: "Putting you through."

Handler: "South London Ambulance Service."

Caller: "A girl just tried to drown herself...I need help!"

Handler: "Is she unconscious?"

Caller: "Yes, she is!"

Handler: "Is the patient breathing?"

Caller: "I don't know! Help me!"

Handler: "I need you to stay really calm. Where are you now?"

Caller: "Cradisfield Park, off Cradisfield Crescent. Please come quickly!"

Handler: "We're sending an ambulance now. Stay on the phone with me."

Caller: "Please come quickly! What if she's dead?"

Handler: "What's your name, please?"

Caller: "Emily."

Handler: "How old are you, sweetheart?"

Caller: "I'm 14."

Handler: "And who is the patient, and what happened?"

Caller [sobbing]: "She's a girl from my school! I saw her jump into an icy pond and I dragged her out. Please come soon!"

Chapter 27

Ellen

I wanted to hold her hand. Tell her it was OK, and that everything would be fine.

In just a few seconds, everything had changed.

It was Monday morning, the first day back after the desolate Christmas holidays. The sky was a sheet of grey, imprisoning any flicker of light in its depths, smothering all the joy in a fog of uncertainty that no eyes could see through.

I was sitting with Amy at the kitchen table, a pen grasped in my hand, whilst I attempted again and again to understand the numbers in front of me as they danced on the page. School had requested that every Monday for half a term I was to have online maths coaching in the morning at home, so Amy could sit and know how to help me.

I heard the phone ring. Amy sighed.

"I shouldn't be a minute, Ellen," she said hastily to me. "Carry on with that worksheet if you can. The tutor is there if you need," she said as she went to answer the phone.

I stared at the laptop screen and at Miss Parson, an old fish-faced woman dug up from some top, free SENCO tuition school. I couldn't concentrate on what she was telling me.

I saw the colour drain out of Amy's face, tears silently sliding down her cheeks.

"Zoe? Are you sure?"

She looked desperate. My heart started banging anxiously. What had happened?

"Yes...yes...I...I'll be there!" she sobbed, her legs buckling in shock.

"Tim! Tim!" she screamed.

Tim ran down the stairs in his pyjama bottoms, shaving foam on his chin, mimicking a Santa beard. This normally would have been comical, but I could see this was no time to be laughing.

"We need to go to the hospital now! It's Zoe!"

"Oh God! What on earth has happened?"

"Just get in the car. I'll explain. We need to go." And she ran to the car, Tim following, hastily putting on a shirt and rinsing his face at the kitchen sink, with me following on after.

Tim and Amy tried to talk in hushed tones, but I could hear. I still failed to understand. Why would Zoe do this? Jump into an icy pond...drown herself?

Oh God!

When we got to the hospital entrance, Amy didn't bother to park, abandoning the car in front of the door and running in, forgetting about me. I ran after them, desperately.

Oh Zoe, what have you done?

A lady behind a desk, looking grave, led Tim and Amy into an office where a grim-faced man sat, everything about him grey. I tried to follow, but they wouldn't let me. I wanted Zoe, and for the first time in months I found the old emotion hitting me again. I wanted mum.

I didn't care what they thought. I had to know if Zoe was OK, so I ran to the door, ear pressed to the crack.

"Mr and Mrs Brown, I am afraid I have grave news concerning your daughter."

Tears stung my eyes and I clenched my fists.

"She was dragged out of a freezing pond this morning. An ambulance team got to her as quickly as they could."

Please let Zoe be OK.

"She was extremely hypothermic, and in the ambulance she suffered a brief cardiac arrest from the shock. CPR was performed, and your daughter recovered her breathing, but I am afraid she is in a coma showing no signs of consciousness. We will do everything we can for her."

The walls collapsed in on me and I screamed. I had already lost my own sister. I couldn't lose Zoe as well!

I crumpled to the floor, shattered again.

Amy and Tim came out of the room, both of them sobbing, distraught. We didn't have to say anything. We just had a long, dejected embrace, united in our pain.

Chapter 28

Zoe

As soon as the darkness came, I felt a sense of light. Peace and acceptance; every pain of my past evaporated.

I saw my life play out before my eyes. Every strong memory, and all the memories I had forgotten.

I didn't know how old I was. I could just feel the hazy warmth of fresh cotton sheets and soft skin. Even then, I didn't feel happy. There was a sense of restlessness, pain and longing.

It was a hot day. I knew this because the earth was dry and baked beneath my scrabbling fingers. I could hear the other children playing, but I was alone. I didn't want to play in the Wendy house, with the bricks, or in the sandpit. I went off to the corner of the garden and searched in the earth there. I wasn't looking for treasure. I was digging for worms. I could feel their slimy bodies clutched in my hot palm. Every time I came across one, I put it in my pocket. I didn't want to play with the other children, and they probably didn't want to play with me.

On my first day of school, I was crying. The shirt didn't feel right, and I didn't want to go into this strange new world of running, screaming children. I held mum's hand and didn't want to talk to anyone. When the teacher tried to lead me inside, I screamed and grasped on to mum, digging my fingers into the wool of her jumper.

In Year 2, a girl from my class came skipping into school with a paper bag of invitations to her 'unicorn birthday party'. Everyone got an invite. Everyone but me.

"Why didn't you invite me?" I remember asking, confused and upset, not yet realising the full reality that I had no friends. The girl smirked and tossed her sleek blonde hair.

"Because you're weird," she replied.

It was PE, and the teacher asked us to get into pairs. Our class was an odd number, and guess who didn't have a partner!

I walked out to the middle of the court on the teacher's command, everybody staring and whispering. I felt my cheeks grow hot.

Why didn't I have a partner?

The teacher made me join up in a three with two other girls. I don't remember their features, but I do recall that they sighed and whispered as I approached.

I was playing with Ava. It felt safe and happy. I couldn't gauge how old we were. I think it was in Year 6. I was at her house in her room, both of us sitting cross-legged on her bed in our school uniforms, making friendship bracelets.

"You will always be my best friend, Zoe," she had said, and embraced me warmly.

Sally's fur felt warm against my head, and I curled up in her dog basket. Her breathing consisted of heavy sighs.

I don't know why I was crying, but I could almost feel the warmth and raspiness of Sally's tongue as she licked my face.

The peaceful feeling faded. I was crying. Crying as I felt the life fade from her body. Hot tears of anger and betrayal streaming down my face.

I could feel frustration. Anger. Neglect.

The moment kept playing over and over again. I could feel the sensation of sheer sadness rise within me, searching for a way out. My hands flailed and punched again and again. I knocked things flying and hit out.

"I never stole the money!" I was screaming. But nobody would listen. Nobody cared.

I felt as I was jerked out of reality. I felt truly free, as if floating. But somehow, this didn't feel quite right.

I felt the padding of paws beside me and turned round to see what it was, and there, stood in front of me, was Sally. Regal and surreal, she walked freely towards me. I let my tears be taken by her fur, and she looked up at me with those big, brown eyes, telling me it was OK.

I was suddenly hit with a torrent of memories, but this time they were joyous.

I saw myself running along the beach in Islay, collecting shells whilst mum and dad chased after me, each one of us laughing.

I saw Ellen and I cuddled up on the sofa watching Netflix, laughing as we gossiped.

I saw mum, dad and me playing a mad game of 'football', rolling over and over in the summer grass in the park.

I saw Ellen playing to me on her cello.

I saw us all boating on the pond last summer.

I saw us all, happy and together, and it was then I realised.

"I'm not ready to die," I whispered into Sally's delicate ear, and she looked up at me with those big brown eyes one last time, knowing I had made the right decision.

She licked my face before elegantly walking into the distance.

I knew I may never see Sally again, but I also knew what I needed to do.

I will never know whether this was an actual experience, or a dream in my head, for thankfully, I wasn't brain-dead.

Suddenly, everything faded back and the noise of reality hit my ears. The noise was contorted and distant, although I was underwater.

Where was I?

The only part of me that seemed to be working were my ears.

I could hear a wailing noise. A distorted cacophony of voices and sirens dancing around me.

I tried to move, but my body seemed to be trapped.

Was somebody trapping me?

I could feel hands on my chest, banging it, and the sensation of some sort of mask on my face.

I gasped for air and the banging stopped.

"She's back!" I heard a relieved voice say.

"Oh, thank God!"

The second voice sounded familiar.

I tried desperately to open my eyes to see who it was. I tried so hard, but it felt like an avalanche had fallen on my eyes.

Was I dead?

My heart raced with the most sheer panic I had ever experienced.

Help me!

I tried to move, to sit up, to show them I was OK. But my body was stiff and heavy, and I failed to move it. Almost as if I were paralysed.

What was happening to me?

I tried to open my mouth to yell out. But no sound came.

Why couldn't I move?

Where was I?

I couldn't remember what had happened. Just the sensation of water. Ice. Emptiness.

I felt somebody holding my hand, clasping my fingers. I tried to open my eyes and failed again.

"I am so, so sorry, Zoe. Please don't die. I want to make everything right. I honestly wish I could go back. Take back all of the hateful words. Undo all of my terrible actions. I wish so much. Please get better, Zoe!" sobbed the voice.

I strained again to remember who I could connect the sound to, but I faltered and another darkness pulled me away.

Chapter 29

Ellen

"Zoe, can you hear me?" I whispered into her ear.

Zoe didn't move. Her black hair was fanned out on the pillow around her, and what I could see of her thin face looked pale and pinched, and yet at ease, almost like she was in an eternal sleep. I couldn't properly see her expression. She had an oxygen mask over her face, and tubes snaking in and out of her body, all connected to beeping, monitoring machinery.

"Do you think she can hear me?" I asked Amy.

"We don't know, Ellen. She might be able to, and it could really help her, but we just don't know," Amy replied, sadly.

I felt for her hand under the sheets and clasped her bony fingers to my heart.

"You will get better, Zoe."

We went to the hospital every day.

Tim and Amy wanted me to stay with Naomi, but I was adamant. I sat by her bed, held her hand, and talked to her all about the things I was doing, trying my hardest to be upbeat. Zoe didn't move.

"Zoe, please will you open your eyes for me?" I whispered into her hair.

Nothing.

"Please, Zoe!" I begged, starting to cry.

"Look, you don't even have to open your eyes. Just move your arm or talk back. I just want you to be OK, Zoe," I sobbed.

We visited Zoe week after week. Every time I would wait by her bed, looking desperately for any sign of response. Amy and Tim tried to be optimistic, but nobody could enlighten me.

I just wanted Zoe back. I had known her for scarcely a few months. However, our bond had formed and become strong, and now she was leaving me.

After many weeks of bitter yearning, Zoe still hadn't changed, and Amy and Tim had a meeting with the doctor. I couldn't listen outside this time because they refused to let me go to the hospital. However, they sat me down and talked to me later that day.

"Ellen, we all love Zoe, very, very much," said Amy, gently, fighting back her emotion.

I didn't want to hear what she had to say.

"She WILL get better!" I said, determinedly.

Tim shook his head sadly, tears silently cascading down his cheeks.

"We all want Zoe to get better, Ellen, but the doctor says we just can't know. Some people don't ever wake up. We can't promise that Zoe will come back, Ellen."

I couldn't bear to hear it. I wouldn't. I needed Zoe.

I screamed in pain and devastation because all my hopes and dreams were gone. There was no spark of light in the darkness. Everything was gone.

I had been having counselling every week previously, and had slowly started to feel better, but now I refused to talk at the sessions, just screaming in hollering pain.

I was only living part-time with the Browns, until it progressed to just weekends, which were mostly spent at Zoe's bedside. One evening on a weekend, I heard the Browns having a fight.

"Think of Ellen, Amy! That poor girl has little to nothing and you already want to snatch that away from her!"

"I just can't live like this any more! It's too much! Everything's too much. We just can't continue to foster her!"

"But she's part of the family now!"

"You always favoured her - maybe that's why all this happened! Zoe is our own daughter!"

"And Zoe is basically dead, Amy!"

"How dare you say that!"

"The least we can do is something positive in our lives, instead of day-in and out at the bedside of the husk of our daughter. This false hope is no good for anybody," Tim said as he broke down. "Don't you dare think I don't love my daughter. She means the whole fucking world to me! Think what she would want."

"I know. I know," Amy sobbed, defeated. "But it's not forever, and right now, it's doing nobody any good. I'm going to ring her social worker tomorrow."

That night I was swallowed by a pit of darkness, silently soaking my pillow. I wanted to scream and break things because my world was so broken; I had nothing. Not only had I lost my sister, but now it looked as if I had lost the entire foundation of my new life. Forever. And now I was falling, falling, falling.

Zoe's room was so ordinary and untouched it was almost like she hadn't gone. School jumpers and bras were strewn across the back of a chair, paper and notebooks all over her desk - a complete contrast to her bed and table, which were neatly made and organised. I pulled back the covers and curled up. Zoe was always paranoid about cleanliness and had showers twice, or even three times a day, often walking around like a ghost, her hair dripping down her back. The smell of her coconut shampoo and soap still lingered on the duvet, and I breathed in deeply.

I suddenly heard a squeak and a scrabble in the room and sat up abruptly. But it was only Zoe's gerbils. When I first came to stay, she had taken each one out of the tank and introduced them to me, taking the time to list each one's name, personality and colouring as if she could never be bored by the subject.

I walked over to them. Luna was chewing at the mesh of the tank and squeaking indignantly. As she heard my footsteps, she stopped, and looked up at me inquiringly. Zoe always said gerbils were very interesting creatures, different from normal pets.

"Do you want feeding?" I asked her.

I felt stupid talking to a gerbil, but Zoe always did.

Luna squeaked again.

I dug my hand into the packet of gerbil food and scattered it in the cage, watching as they all surrounded it, taking it piece by piece to their nest. At least they had each other, even if they didn't have Zoe. I felt truly alone.

I brought in my cello case. I felt too empty to play, so I just sat, stroking the varnished wood whilst the emotion cascaded down my face. Then I stopped. I saw a piece of folded notepaper in my case, almost as if it had been precisely placed there. It was printed 'Ellen' in Zoe's spidery handwriting. Hands trembling in cold sweat, I unfolded it, afraid of what I might find.

'If I die, tell mum and dad how much I loved them.

Please remember my decisions weren't because of you. Brush my hair out in my coffin for me Ellen, and play pop music at my funeral, but please don't be sad. Your lives are better off this way. Look after

mum and dad for me. Know that I will always love you; I just don't love my life any more. Make mum and dad proud. You can be a much better daughter for them than I could ever be. Zoe'

I hadn't been aware I'd been crying all this time whilst Zoe's words echoed around my head.

Chapter 30

Zoe

I was screaming. Every emotion and will inside me fighting to show them. I was going to get better, whatever they said.

Mum, dad and Ellen came to visit me every day. These were the most important people in my life, so I should've enjoyed their visits the most. However, I always dreaded them. They would sit around me and talk awkwardly, any meaning to their words drowned out by sadness. I was so desperate to talk to them. To open my eyes. Squeeze Ellen's hand back. Show them I was still Zoe, even if I was trapped in this useless body. I just lay there, a terrified wreck. Screaming to connect to the outside world.

I'm still Zoe!

I CAN hear you!

I AM HERE!

Listen to me!

All I wanted to do was go back in time to make things right. How could I have been so insane?

I thought I would find peace, but it vanished as soon as it came. I was back. Trapped in this new reality.

I heard footsteps approaching my bed. I thought it would be mum, dad and Ellen again, and braced myself for another painful visit, but these were new, yet familiar voices.

"Zoe?" said one girl as she sat by my bed.

"Zoe, it's Ava!"

Ava? AVA!

Anger raged inside me as I saw all the horrible memories before my eyes once again.

'Why didn't you invite me?'

'I didn't invite you because you're a FREAK, Zoe!'

'I never stole the money. It was all a frame.'

I wanted to turn away from her, but she clutched my hand tight. I wanted to wrench it away, but I was imprisoned. Immobile. A vegetable.

I felt the mattress dip as somebody sat on the end of the bed.

"Zoe..." said the voice, a little more tentatively than Ava.

"Zoe. I am so...so...sorry!" she said, her voice choked up with past guilt.

Emily?

Suddenly the fog cleared, and I remembered. The girl holding my hand. She told me not to die. She had...saved me? Emily...?

"Zoe, I can't go back, but we can go forward - together. I am a changed person, Zoe. I'm sorry."

I felt her words sink into my soul, filling my depths with passion and unlocking a chain.

Let me out!

A tear trickled down my cheek.

"Oh Zoe!" sobbed Ava. "Can you hear us?"

"Zoe!" cried Emily, as she clutched my hand even tighter.

"Zoe, I need you to open your eyes for me - or talk. Squeeze my hand or something. I need to know you are OK."

I don't think I had ever felt such frustration in my life. It was terrifying, not being in control of my own body. Imprisoned. Drowned.

I did the only thing I could. I inhaled deeply and let it go.

"Nurse! Doctor!" shouted Emily, desperately.

I heard the sound of more footsteps, squeaky on the polished hospital floor.

"Look!" said Ava.

I think she was pointing to my wet cheeks.

"And she sighed! Really loudly!"

I felt my eyelids being opened, and could make out a blur of a light, although it was extremely hazy. The nurse took a deep breath.

"Girls, I know you want Zoe to get better. We all do. However, there is no evidence she is conscious. Sighing can be involuntary. Her pupils aren't responding to light," said the nurse, briskly.

"What about her crying? Surely that shows emotion?" retorted Emily.

"Again, comatose patients may laugh, cry or even smile, and in most cases these moments are involuntary."

And I heard the sound of retreating footsteps.

"Don't listen to them, Zoe," croaked Emily. "You ARE going to get better!"

I am going to get better.

I am going to break free.

I am a fighter.

Chapter 31

Ellen

It had been 10 weeks. I crossed every day off on my calendar. Every visit as painful as the last.

A few times, when I had woken up in the darkest despair in the night, I would slide out of my own bed and curl up in Zoe's, and it eased the pain, just that little bit.

As much as I tried to convince myself, I couldn't stop that spidery writing of truth being scrawled across my head.

One night, I heard Tim and Amy having a sobbed conversation in the kitchen when they thought I was asleep.

"Oh God, I just can't bloody live like this any more."

Amy was bent over in a chair; her head in her hands, her posture the image of distress.

"I just want her back!"

"I know, and she might still get better. We have to be positive. It's the only way," Tim wept, trying to compose himself.

"Tim, the hospital says she has a 5% chance! And even then, she'll probably have brain damage," Amy sobbed into her hands. "How are we going to say this to

Ellen? She's had enough damage in her life as it is. She's only known Zoe for a few months, yet I can see how much they've grown to love each other.

"I know this sounds so defeatist, but I don't know any other way to say it. We've got to start thinking of the future. Of *Ellen.* We can't be yearning forever. We have to start making plans. Can we really continue to foster her? We have given the girl love and a new start, but perhaps it's time for her to move on as well," said Amy.

Those words hit me like an electric shock, sending sparks of anger sizzling through me, and I ran into the kitchen.

I also felt guilt flush me as I remembered Zoe's note.

Should I show it to them?

NO.

It would make everything too *real.*

But now I had this new knot of knowledge in my stomach, knowing Zoe's accident may not have been an accident.

I couldn't bear it.

The foundations had been broken, and I would become a loose parcel, forced out and chucked from home to home.

"You CAN'T forget Zoe! She is going to get better! Didn't you hear what the hospital said? She sighed and cried! I know she is there. We can't just give up on her! She's had too much of that already."

I stared up at Amy and Tim through a stream of water. "Everyone has always given up on Zoe."

But whether I liked it or not, as the days went by, Zoe was becoming a memory.

Then I knew exactly what I needed to do, and it might just be the missing piece.

I picked up my cello and lumbered out of the door.

Chapter 32

Zoe

Count to 100. Do it now. Don't miss out any numbers.

No use.

200...300...400.

Why can't I wake up?

500...1,000.

Gabble 'wake up' inside your head, 50 times.

200 times...400 times.

Scream! Tell them you're OK. You're still Zoe, no matter what.

I couldn't talk.

I couldn't wake up.

If I had to describe the one emotion, the feeling that was with me every second of the day, the feeling that caused me pain, the feeling I had no power over...it was the feeling of fear.

Fear and regret.

I knew all too well what was going to happen. It was a race against time.

I would be put into a care home. Talked about as a memory. Forgotten, and in the past.

If people hardly noticed me normally, how on earth could I make them see me now?

I just lay there, whilst the hours ticked by.

Emily came to visit me every day, without fail. And every day, another piece of the story was unravelled.

"I wish it was me on that bed instead of you, Zoe. I deserve it," she started, bitterly, squeezing my hand.

"Sometimes I can pretend I have a reason - and by God, I wish to heck I did?" she sighed.

"Truth is, Zoe, you were always right. We were all bitches, just because we liked the power," she said.

I felt a drop of water land on my cheek. A *tear*. I felt it sink into my skin and fill every inch of my body with passion. That one tear drop contained so many emotions. Compassion. Anger. Longing. Guilt.

"Please, Zoe, open your eyes. Show that you know I'm sorry. Forgive me, Zoe."

I had to wake up.

WAKE THE HELL UP, ZOE!

I AM HERE.

HELP ME.

I AM ZOE.

Every hair on my body stood up in tension and I felt a wave of anger surge through me.

I opened my eyes.

But it wasn't enough.

Chapter 33

Ellen

"Ellen! Ellen, wait!" shouted Amy as she and Tim ran after me into the night.

"We need to go to the hospital!" I shouted.

"Ellen! Come inside now!" commanded Tim.

But I took no notice.

"I'm sorry. I need to go to the hospital *now*. I need to see Zoe."

I ran down the road as fast as I could, with my cello on my back. I heard them running after me, shouting, panting.

But I wasn't listening.

My mind was on one thing. Zoe.

I remembered all the times I had played to her before. How it had soothed and healed her.

"Ellen! Stop!"

I had to carry on.

"They won't let you see Zoe at this time!"

Yes they would.

"Ellen! Please stop!"

Carry on, Ellen, run. For Zoe.

I ran and ran, dirty rainwater splattering my legs. But I carried on determinedly.

Nearly there now.

I felt myself trip and fell to the ground, my cello case landing on top of me with a thud. Winded and lying there.

"Oh my goodness! I'm so sorry!" said a voice I vaguely recognised, but the darkness meant I couldn't distinguish the girl's face.

"Are you OK?"

"Yes, yes, I'm fine! Don't worry!"

No.

I wasn't fine.

I needed to tell the truth.

"NO!" I sobbed. "My sister is in hospital! Amy says she is sleeping and she might not wake up!"

I broke down.

The girl crouched down beside me and held my hand.

"My friend is in hospital too. She's in a coma. Everyone keeps telling me that she can't hear me, and she probably won't ever wake up. But I'm going to prove them wrong, because Zoe opened her eyes today. I know that means something, even though all those stupid nurses say it's involuntary."

I stopped, startled.

"Zoe?!"

Zoe opened her eyes?!

Then I heard voices behind me.

"Ellen! Ellen! Thank goodness we found you!" came Amy's panicked voice.

She kneeled beside me and pulled me on to her lap whilst I sobbed into her chest.

"Mum, I need to save Zoe!" I wept.

I felt Amy's arms tighten round me, and I felt safe. Then I realised what I had said - 'Mum'.

"I know, darling, I know."

I heard a car draw up on the kerb and Tim got out and immediately came by my side, and we all had a long embrace.

"Dad," I choked.

Tim looked a little taken aback, and then he smiled.

"Yes, Ellen, we're here!"

The girl stood awkwardly beside us, looking with longing.

"I think I'd better introduce myself," she said, her voice thick.

Then I felt myself flame as I realised from the light of Tim's headlights who she was.

"My name is Emily...", but I cut her off.

"Emily!" I spat, horrified, remembering.

Emily! Emily who had thrown white spirit all over Zoe; called her a loser and a freak, along with many other callous names; stalked her every day with devastating messages; manipulated the situation to make everybody think she was innocent; framed Zoe for stealing money off her best friend. And she had told Zoe to kill herself!

It suddenly clicked.

No. It couldn't be.

Zoe hadn't been trying to drown herself because of Emily...had she?

She had been made to feel so worthless and unloved, thinking she was of no use to anyone.

Emily saw the look on my face and looked deeply ashamed. Then she took my hand, looking at the three of us.

"I'm so, so, sorry!" she choked. "This is all my fault. I have been so nasty to your daughter. I told her to kill herself...," she cut off, sobbing.

"I've been visiting her every day. I think you saw me a couple of times. I was just walking back from the hospital. I would do anything to bring her back. I am so sorry," and she bowed her head in shame.

I'd had too many people let me down in my short life. There was no reason I should forgive her. I didn't want to. But, somehow, I knew it was the right thing to do.

"I don't know why you did the things you did to my sister. Words hurt more than I think you realise. But I also know how you feel - just wanting to make things right. So, I do forgive you, Emily," I said, looking straight into her eyes.

Then I hugged her tight.

She turned to Tim and Amy.

"As soon as Zoe is better - and she *will* get better - I'm handing myself in to the police. I will show them everything. Tell them the truth. I'm sorry."

Tim and Amy were both shocked into silence, and for a good 30 seconds the only sounds in the quiet street were the ticking of Tim's car hazard lights and distant traffic.

Then Amy's phone rang.

I couldn't hear who she was talking to, but I could see her face. The blood drained from her cheeks, and her jaw shook. She closed her eyes and shuddered. I felt my throat close up, the buildings collapsed on top of me, and I lay on the pavement shaking, not wanting to hear a word. I couldn't blot out the sobs and howls from Tim and Amy.

No. No. No. It's not true.

"Ellen..." said Tim, trying to compose himself.

"No!" I sobbed as I hit the ground.

"Ellen...please listen," he said so imploringly that I had to look him in the eyes. They were bloodshot and devastated.

"Ellen, Zoe's...not very well," he said delicately. "She stopped breathing again. The hospital did everything they could, darling. Zoe is on life support."

"We might have to say goodbye to Zoe," wept Amy.

"No!" sobbed Emily. "It can't be! Zoe WILL get better!"

"WE'RE NOT TOO LATE!" I screamed.

"Ellen, please listen to me," said Amy.

"NO! You've all given up on Zoe! Well, I haven't! I'm going to the hospital now and you can't stop me!"

Before I could march off with my cello, Tim put his hand on my shoulder.

"You're right, Ellen. Let's go to the hospital now."

Tim drove all of us in his car, whilst Emily tapped out urgent messages on her phone.

"Who are you texting?" I asked.

"A couple of people that need to be with us, Ellen."

I was confused.

Who else needed to see Zoe now?

Why couldn't it just be Tim, Amy and me?

When we arrived, Tim went straight up to the front desk.

"Please, I know it's not visiting time..."

"I apologise, Sir, but I can't let you in. Come back tomorrow between two and eight."

"Look, my daughter is on life support. She is hanging on to life by a thread. We NEED to see her, and it might just help her!"

The receptionist softened.

"Oh, Zoe Brown?" she said sadly in a lowered voice, patting Tim's shoulder. "She's in a private room being monitored. Go along the corridor, to the first floor. Room 7, to your left," and she turned her back on us so we could slip away.

Tim had to beg another nurse, who was monitoring Zoe. But eventually, she let us in.

At first, I didn't recognise the girl on the bed. She had an oxygen mask over her face and even more tubes and machines wired up to her. The only way I knew this stranger really was Zoe was by the wispy black hair, fanned out on her pillow.

"Oh, Zoe!" said Amy, and she sat beside her, stroking stray locks off her face. "Mummy's here!"

Emily stayed by the door, squeezed her eyes shut and I saw hot tears slip down her cheeks. I knew how she felt, so I went over.

"We'll go together," I said, leading her over to Zoe.

Emily and I both held her hand.

Just then, the door to the room swung open and two people rushed in. One was a girl with long, shiny brown hair, followed by an older woman that must have been her mum.

It was Ava.

"Did we make it?" asked the girl, panicked.

"Yes, come and sit down."

Ava's mum walked over to Amy and they had a long embrace as they both tried to be strong.

"Come and sit down," said Tim.

So, there we all were, sitting on hard hospital chairs, surrounding Zoe, all peering at her expectantly. Each one of us willing her to wake up. Zoe just lay there, each beep and wheeze of the machines reminding us that time was running out. I knew it was now or never.

I went to my cello case and carefully eased out the conker- brown shiny instrument and set up, tuning it first after my fall.

Now or never, Ellen.

And I started to play.

I didn't need the music. All the notes I needed were in front of me, and I played them.

Slow. Desolate.

I knew Tim and Amy had expected me to play bright, happy music. But that wasn't truthful. And even if they didn't see it, I knew Zoe needed the truth.

"I love you so, so much, Zoe. You always make me so proud," choked Tim, and he leant forwards and kissed her on the cheek. He didn't say very much, but sometimes actions say more than words.

"You will always be my best friend, Zoe, and I am so, so sorry about the way I have acted with you recently. I've made you a friendship bracelet. It's your favourite colours, blue and purple. I have one too, so we will be best friends forever."

Ava slid the dainty string bracelet on to Zoe's wrist.

"Oh, Zoe! You're my own daughter. I love you more than life, my darling. Mummy loves you, now and forever," said Amy, and she smoothed back Zoe's hair and gave her a long kiss on the forehead.

"Zoe, I know they have all given up on you," sobbed Emily, clutching her hand. "Zoe, please can you ever forgive me? I am so, so sorry. I know you can do it, Zoe. I believe in you!"

Zoe didn't move. The only sound in the room was the melancholic sound of my strings, and the beeping and monitoring signals of the hospital bedside machines.

"Please," whispered Emily, visibly distressed.

Nothing.

"Please, Zoe."

Please

Nothing.

Then she opened her eyes, looking straight at me, glazed with tears as they trickled silently down, pooling on her oxygen mask. I ran over to her. I saw behind the mask. Behind her mask of scars. The girl, who had been trapped inside...her whole life a mask.

I didn't listen to their screams of joyous relief as they huddled around her bed. It was just me and Zoe, locked and united in our own silent world. She looked at me, her deep blue watery eyes meeting mine in eternal gratitude.

———

Then came a sigh. *Zoe's* sigh, desperately trying to communicate.

More tears tracked and stained her face; not tears of sadness, but tears of strength.

I removed the oxygen mask. Zoe gazed slowly around the room, taking in each and every one of us. Then, slowly summoning every inch of her sudden awakening, she softly mouthed.

"I...forgive...you."

Afterword

Zoe

I want to say thank you.

Thank you that for whatever reason my life was spared that day. I don't know how or why, but thank you that I have a life.

However, most of all, I would like to thank Emily, because it really takes guts to admit your mistakes and apologise. Emily never gave up on me, and neither did Ellen. Thank you so much.

You may be wondering what happened to Emily. I had to have months of rehabilitation, but when I had recovered, she handed herself in to the police. She wanted to punish herself, just like me, but I should know, punishment isn't an apology. The only true act of apology is a change in behaviour.

Mum and dad thought it would be good to make a fresh start in a new home. I thought I would find it hard to move, but somehow, it felt right. South-east London belonged in the past.

Ava said she would stay in touch, but to be honest, I never really saw her again, nor James, Emily or anybody else from my school. We decided to move to the seaside, which was my dream come true. Like I had always secretly hoped, we moved into the old cottage in Islay.

I had always thought it was my fault I couldn't make friends, but I learned that the past hadn't been my fault, and I learned to live and embrace my true colours, behind the mask. In fact, I did make friends. On the first week of moving, we decided to explore the beach further. Ellen and I ran along the shore, splashing each other and laughing. I think that was the first time I discovered what happiness felt like. Such a wonderful, light feeling, my new medication calming the anxiety that used to control my life. There was a girl fishing on the end of the pier. She had abundant black hair that cascaded down to her waist, her tangled locks dancing in the breeze.

"Hello," I whispered.

"We just moved here. We live in the pink cottage on the seafront - the one with primroses in the garden."

"Oh, hello," she said, in her soft Scottish burr.

"Oh, wow! I love that road! I call those houses 'the neapolitans' because they're coloured just like the ice cream! I live only a couple of doors along - the pale yellow one with the roses in the garden. I'm Jade, by the way..,Jade Macintosh," she said and held out her hand, forgetting it was covered in slimy fish guts. Jade laughed, wiping her hands on her tattered dress.

"Sorry! Sorry! I'm just fishing for supper. Want to have a look?"

And from that moment on, I had a friend. Jade taught me to fish and skim stones on the waves. She also had a dog, Rose. She was a Labrador, just like Sally, only chestnut in colour. I told her about Sally, and you'll never guess what...Rose's mum had another litter of puppies, and Morag let us have one. She is this ultra sweet, warm old lady who always gives me stale fruit drops and has become like a grandma to me. I didn't want to name my new dog Sally, because she wasn't Sally. Instead, I decided to call her Emily, so I could keep a little bit of the past. Rose and Emily play together every day, and Jade and I walk to school together. And, best of all, I have a proper sister, Ellen. She is staying with us for a long time! She is doing extremely well on the cello, and sometimes plays it on the beach to the seals.

So, we all live on the isle of Islay. I don't want to say happily ever after, because life doesn't work like that. Some days are good, and occasionally there's a bad day, but overall, I am so much happier. But I could never have done it without my sister, Ellen.

About the Author

Born in late 2009, Bethany Lunney is a teen writer based in Worcestershire who enjoys literature in many forms, such as novels and poetry.

Her writing often reflects topics she feels passionately about, such as equality and justice. As well as writing, she enjoys spending her free time swimming, walking (or anything outdoors) with her Labrador, as well as the arts.

She especially enjoys acting and dreams of acting in a series one day.

Q&A with Bethany Lunney

Why did you want to write a book?

I suppose my mentality is that we only have one life, which could be taken from us at any second. I wanted to make the most out of every opportunity I could to impact the world and others and fulfil my dreams positively. I really wanted to use my perspective to let others know who may be going through things similar to those of the characters in my book that there can always be light and that life as you are living never has to end.

Does writing energise or exhaust you?

Writing is a draining thing, which may surprise some people. However, that doesn't mean that I do not love the process. Writing for me personally feels like words overflowing a dam, as my writing is poured out from weeks or months of building ideas and emotion, so expressing them in the form of words feels very freeing but also draining, as it takes a lot of effort to tessellate so many ideas into something so compact.

What message did you want your book to convey to the reader?

The main message was probably that each comment you make to somebody in your life is like throwing a rock into a lake; you will never know how deep that rock will go. People portray to others only the best parts of themselves twisted into a mask, and behind that, we have no idea what struggles they are hiding. So, in short, just make that effort to be kind and accepting of everybody. It could literally save their life.

What is the first book you read that had a real impact on you, and why?

I hated reading until around the age of 9 because all the books I was introduced to at school didn't light me up. I found my love for reading through a dark place in my life when my mental health first started to go downhill at the age of eight and nine. I was terrified to eat anything as my anxiety was so bad, and so at lunch and often break times at my primary school, I would sit alone and read while everybody ate or played. I loved Jaqueline Wilson's books and probably read nearly all of them back-to-back multiple times. I discovered reading as such an amazing way to escape reality.

More recently, books I have read that left an impact were 'The Kite Runner' by Khaled Hosseini, 'The Lovely Bones' by Alice Sebold, and 'As Long As The Lemon Trees Grow' by Zoulfa Katouh.

How did it feel to hold your book in your hands for the first time?

At this point in my writing, I haven't yet received my novel, but I know it will be surreal and amazing, and I'm sure a tear or two will be shed.

How many other books do you feel you have in you?

I honestly have no idea. With my writing, I very much go with the flow and often like to explore different paths and opportunities in life. When I get inspiration, it is often very sudden and unexpected, so I guess I will just have to see what my future has in store for me.

How much time did you dedicate each day/week to writing your book?

The writing-school-music-sport balance was undoubtedly hard to juggle, so I wrote whenever and wherever possible. One of my most frequent places to write was on my bus journey to school, which is a very dull twenty minutes of my life, and if I were bored in lessons, I would draft ideas in the back of my exercise books. The book consumed my thoughts though, as I was always planning my characters' next paths. A place I would often think of these ideas was swimming training. If it was a long distance set, and it was very easy to get bored-so I would almost disconnect my head to think up scenarios while my body went into auto-pilot to keep lapping up and down. Aside from that, I would type up my ideas at least one evening a week.

How would you deal with a bad review?

I wouldn't really do anything, as I know that isn't my problem. The amazing thing about people is that we all have completely different interests and tastes (wow), which means that we obviously aren't going to like the same things. It goes without saying that not everybody will enjoy my novel, and that is completely okay because if we all had the same favourite book genre...a bookstore would be pretty boring!

Did you suffer from writer's block at any point during the writing process? If so, how did you overcome it?

Yes, I did suffer from writer's block, especially at one point in the process when my book was capped at around 30,000 words, and I knew I had to extend it by at least 20,000 to have any chance of it being worthwhile. To get over it, I expanded the book's timeline by a whole year and came up with more events to explore in my characters' lives.

What are your favourite genre of books to read?

I enjoy reality fiction, semi-autobiographical fiction, and reality novels—anything that has happened or could very likely happen in the current world. I am not, and I have never been, a fan of fantasy or magical novels as much.

Did you find writing a therapeutic experience?

It is a satisfactory experience if your ideas just flow onto the page, but as I said earlier, it is also very hard to write, so it is quite tiring. That is why when I am writing, I find it beneficial to take regular breaks.

What are you doing to ensure that your book stays current and is at the top of people's wish lists?

I am active on my social media pages, especially my Instagram and Facebook (bethanylunney_writes), where I post a lot about my novel and write a wider range of things to engage a larger audience.

What advice would you give to someone considering writing their book?

Don't give up! It is so easy to get disheartened and have a block, as a novel is a massive commitment to finish, but remember that there is no time pressure, and go at your own pace! I started writing my book in early 2022, but it is so worth it when you finally reach the end of the road.

What would you have done differently, if anything, in writing your book?

It probably would've helped me if I had written out a rough timeline from the beginning of the process because I basically carried all of the information in my head, which meant I kept forgetting things and re-remembering them. Other than that, with all the school, life, and writing balance, I am happy with what I achieved.

Are you planning on writing more books similar to your current one, a completely different genre, or is one enough?

Similar to what I said earlier, I have no idea. I am pretty certain, though, that this book will not have a sequel because I know it's time to leave my characters to get on with their 'lives'; my dream would be to have my novel televised in some way as I feel it would make a nice, unique series. Other than that, I will have to see where life takes me.

Printed in Great Britain
by Amazon

57505673R00162